TRACY CROW

COOPER'S HAWK

THE REMEMBERING

D1522252

This book is a work of fiction. Names, characters, places, and incidents either are products of the author's imagination or are used fictitiously. Any resemblance to actual events or locales or persons, living or dead, is entirely coincidental.

"Morning Has Broken," from Children's Bells by Eleanor Farjeon, reprinted with permission from Oxford University Press.

Copyright © 2018 by PipeVine Press an Imprint of Warren Publishing

All rights reserved. This book may not be reproduced or stored in whole or in part by any means without the written permission of the author except for brief quotations for the purpose of review.

ISBN: 978-1-943258-63-5
Library of Congress Catalog Number: 2017963837
Crow. Tracy.
Cooper's Hawk: The Remembering

Edited by: Jessica Carelock

Published by PipeVine Press
an Imprint of Warren Publishing

Charlotte, NC
www.pipevinepress.com
www.warrenpublishing.net
Printed in the United States

Cover and interior design by Mindy Kuhn

FORTHCOMING BOOKS BY TRACY CROW & PIPEVINE PRESS

The Heart Navigator, the prequel to *Cooper's Hawk*, is forthcoming in fall 2018.

After the combat death of his father and the accidental death of his mother, an angry and disheartened sixteen-year-old Willis is forced to live with the grandfather who turned his back on the family when his son chose a wife outside the family's Native American heritage. During their turbulent transition with each other, Grandfather White Feather receives a vision, and soon he and Willis set out to retrace the Trail of Tears. Along this yearlong journey, Grandfather relies on the natural world to reveal the lessons the boy needs for repairing his broken heart. And Willis teaches his shaman-grandfather about the meaning of unconditional love—and about the man, woman, and grandson his grandfather abandoned for sixteen years because of pride.

The Collaborator, the sequel to *Cooper's Hawk*, is forthcoming in fall 2019.

After a cataclysmic earthquake in California and worldwide turmoil caused by the deconstruction of democracies and socialism, world leaders finally converge on a new island nation in the Pacific, where they receive leadership counsel from *the boy*, Elijah Condor, who has successfully formed the world's first leaderless society, governed through the art of collaboration. With the help of his shaman-Merlin guide Willis, the boy—who possesses the Knowing that will change the world—teaches that the only successful, future form of government that can co-exist with the new elegance of consciousness is one designed and led by skillful, master collaborators.

Accept Your Gifts, a spirituality-based memoir, is forthcoming in summer 2019.

After a painful, humiliating divorce from husband-number-three, Tracy embarks on a nine-year spiritual journey—one compelling an extensive self-study of world religions and otherworldly spiritual belief systems. Through a series of unusual synchronicities, Tracy's journey culminates with the six-week writing experience of *Cooper's Hawk*, and leads her toward a future she has never imagined for herself.

Nothing is ever as it seems.

PRAISE FOR
COOPER'S HAWK

"Extremely engaging...Such heart and energy and voice—all of which unfolds with confidence and purity...It's been a long time since a book has moved me this much."

— Jeffery Hess, author of *Beachhead* and *Cold War Canoe Club*

"Cooper's Hawk introduces us to veteran-patients who rely on their VA hospital for their health, their sanity, and their community...and reveals the beauty in their struggles and the magic in their tragedy. Bottom line, you cannot get through this book without feeling something deeply."

— M.L. Doyle, co-author of the Shoshana Johnson memoir,
I'm Still Standing: From Captive U.S. Soldier to Free Citizen—My Journey Home,
and author of *The Bonding Spell* and *The Peacekeeper's Photograph*

"'What do you imagine happens to a man when he finally faces the truth about the Divinity within his enemy?' In Cooper's Hawk, Tracy Crow explores the divinity within all of us, the places where we shirk from seeing it, or where we long to. A work of great compassion, open-hearted and unflinching, Cooper's Hawk provides the fodder for ample discussion about what it means to survive, to heal, and to forgive."

— Andria Williams, author of *The Longest Night*

"With this novella, Tracy Crow has created a world that transports readers into VA hospital rooms and into the cemetery beyond, with all the psychological freight that this implies. Even more, Crow's fiction returns us to the world we live in—and to ourselves within it…."

— Brian Turner, author of *My Life As A Foreign Country: A Memoir* and *Here, Bullet*

"If you've ever wondered about the invisible wounds of war, you'll want to read this book. With the warmth of a storyteller and clarity of perspective only a cultural insider can offer, Tracy Crow takes us into a world few will ever know—though the connections matter to us all."

— Kate Hendricks Thomas, PhD, author of *Brave, Strong, True: The Modern Warrior's Battle for Balance* and *Bulletproofing the Psyche*

"Deeply touching…the transformative messages of hope and healing within Cooper's Hawk convey an unforgettable resonance."

— CJ Scarlet, life coach and author of *The Badass Girl's Guide: Uncommon Strategies to Outwit Predators*

"A deeply spiritual meditation on compassion, creativity, the natural world, and human connection. In Cooper's Hawk, Tracy Crow goes beyond tales of individual suffering in the aftermath of war to consider the nature of moral injury, the possibility of redemption, and the ways in which we make meaning from traumatic experience."

— Jerri Bell, managing editor of *O-Dark-Thirty* and co-author of *It's My Country Too: Women's Military Stories from the American Revolution to Afghanistan*

ACKNOWLEDGMENTS

Everything becomes material for a writer, I have often joked to friends and family.

Never has this been truer than during the writing of *Cooper's Hawk,* a story inspired by actual events. To those who trusted me with the stories that made their way into this book after a yearlong tour of my text, *On Point: A Guide to Writing the Military Story,* thank you.

At one stop during the book tour, an army veteran had been standing in line for some time to talk to me after a speech. When it was his turn, he thrust a letter in my hand, and said, "I took this from the body of a Viet Cong soldier I was forced to kill in hand-to-hand combat—my first kill too." His eyes were forming large pools. Mine were fast catching up. I glanced down at the envelope that contained the mysterious letter, and heard him say, "Please see to it this letter finds a way into the world. I know you'll find a way."

And for a year, stories like this one fluttered toward me— sometimes through phones calls such as the story surrounding *Charlie,* though the actual story ended tragically for the colonel and his family—and sometimes in person, such as the day I met the real-life Battle of the Bulge poet who lives near Asheville, North Carolina. When he told me about his grandson's suicide in Germany, I felt my legs buckle. "You'll find a way to get this story in the world."

I had no idea at the time that I was already on a journey toward writing *Cooper's Hawk*—at least not consciously. I can see it all so clearly, of course, now. How I've been on this journey toward *Cooper's Hawk* for nearly nine years.

To my dear friends and fellow spiritual seekers within our Journey to the Self class led by Sam and Novella Kennedy in Liberty, North Carolina—thank you for your unwavering encouragement and trust. To Novella—my *most* heartfelt thanks and gratitude for introducing me to *Willis*.

Certainly no one has been more supportive throughout my writing life than Jeffery Hess, a Navy veteran, novelist, founder and leader of the DD-214 Writers' Workshop in Tampa, Florida, and editor of two award-winning volumes of military fiction. Thank you, Dear Friend.

I'd also like to thank the following friends and fellow writers who provided immeasurable encouragement along the writing journey of this book: Catherine Barker, Jerri Bell, Mary Doyle, Maria Edwards, Elizabeth Torres Evans, Jill Renee Feeler, Brooke King, Margaret MacInnis, Andi Madden, Stephanie Massengale, Amber Mathwig, Diane Nine, Libby Oberg, Kathleen M. Rodgers, CJ Scarlet, Elizabeth Tomaselli, Antoinette Lee Toscano, Brian Turner, Andria Williams, and Kayla Williams.

While I have never met the talented Australian pianist and composer, Fiona Joy Hawkins, I feel compelled to publicly acknowledge the depth of creative inspiration I received from her album, Angel Above My Piano—in particular her songs, *Thinking of You* and *Love Forever* (2nd Movement Opus for Love)—which I kept on loop during each writing session of *Cooper's Hawk*. Thank you, Fiona Joy.

Deep gratitude goes out to the many former colleagues and students at the University of Tampa, Eckerd College, and Queens University of Charlotte who continue to offer all sorts of support.

To Malinda (Mindy) Kuhn, Amy Ashby, and the entire team at PipeVine Press, a special thanks for believing in this book, and in me. Co-creating with you has been the most exhilarating experience of my writing life.

Lastly, what would I be without family? For you especially—Mark, Morgan, Brian, Polly, Vern, and Mike—thank you for sustaining me with unconditional love.

CHAPTER 1

The boy is coming.

WHILE he waits for the boy to show, he wheels the janitorial cart toward the east dining room and parks it. Facing a wall of windows he cleaned the night before, the man known as Willis inspects his work. This time of day—thanks to the expanding sunrise over the Cooper VA National Cemetery at the bottom of the dew-slick hill, less than a football field's distance from the hospital—every streak left behind, every smudge overlooked the night before under artificial lighting, will now be exposed. A second chance to fix a mistake is a gift.

Behind him, the murmuring crowd of hospital caregivers retreats toward darker corners with their breakfast trays, coffee, and feeble greetings. Willis stoically faces the east and waits, his thoughts once again returning to the boy. What he doesn't yet know about the boy far outweighs what he does know, but this is nothing new. He suspects the boy will look like his father, but questioning why the boy is coming for Willis is pointless. Everything is revealed in its own time.

Take *his* mistakes, for example, now that the sun has burst above the stone columned entrance of the twenty-two-acre cemetery. Willis scans each pane of glass. In one hand he holds a spray bottle of cleaner and a wad of white paper towels. Usually a ninety-degree wedge of a window pane here and there along the expansive wall of glass demands his extra attention. This morning is no different. "Got to remind me *every* day to stay humble," he jokes, and attacks first the likely nose print from a veteran's service dog, or perhaps a child's since he's also missed the tell-tale tiny fingerprints at the bottom of a lower pane. Seems every day more service dogs, more kids. Vets are getting younger, more women vets are appearing, and the number of older vets is dwindling every week. Dove Jennings and Harold Jay are hanging in there still, but every day fewer and fewer old soldiers, sailors, airmen, and Marines in their wheelchairs form the smoking circles on the patio behind the cafeteria to swap stories about being young and stupid and scared, and to compare injuries and gripes about the Cooper VA. Those who do show up for the smoking circles make for a colorful lot. They sport VFW pins like medals on their vests, or wear whatever uniform clothing they have left that still fits—a camouflaged jacket too small to be buttoned can always be worn over a T-shirt.

When Willis finishes, he steps back to take another wide look at the glass wall. Satisfied, he returns the spray bottle to his cart and tosses the paper towels in a large trash container that he'll be back to empty after three, because everyone flocks to this east dining room after the sun moves overhead. In a few hours, hospital workers, volunteers, and visitors will begin the transfiguration of this room, angling every table and chair he straightened with military precision during the night for the best possible view.

You see, the hummingbirds had been his idea, or so his favorite nurse has, unfortunately, told everyone at the Cooper VA. When he received the invitation to work here months earlier in winter, he had overheard a handful of complaints about the view of the Cooper National Cemetery—how the view of a cemetery was an insensitive reminder of where a loved one upstairs in hospice care was soon headed. The site planning sixty-eight years earlier had involved a monetary kickback to the architect for turning a blind eye, so to speak, at how best to incorporate the valley's western view of the majestic Blue Ridge mountain range. What would have been an uplifting view for families gathered in the dining room for coffee while waiting out the word of a loved one's surgery, or an opportune healing view for the one-hundred-eighty-nine patient rooms had been wasted on hospital administrators and individual offices provided to doctors. Willis, however, enjoys each resplendent sunset view from the offices he tidies during early evenings, and draws on this impactful energy in the west to perfect his plan for spring at the Cooper VA. At times he catches himself, and chides himself for, wasting mindful energy on what he cannot change, such as wishing he had the strength to lift and turn the whole VA operation around—a full one-eighty. If left to him, he'd shake up the whole place. But it's not up to him. Not all of it anyway. Still, the administrators and doctors enjoying their nearer-to-God daytime mountain views might realize their earthly purposes a whole lot faster if they had to stare out over the thirty-eight thousand dead buried at the National Cemetery as Cooper VA patients and visitors are expected to do.

When spring finally rolled down the mountains, warming and greening the valley, Willis enacted his most creative project ever. He started by installing several hummingbird feeders and two small gurgling bird baths outside the east dining room. He planted a flower garden, too, of coral bells, morning glories, lantana, gardenia bushes, several varieties of roses, and a butterfly bush he's still wishing he had bought larger and two of. Willis never asked permission to dig up the earth within the horseshoe shadow of the two red-brick, cemetery-facing towers; he never asks permission to do anything at the Cooper VA. Willis enjoys full autonomy. Nobody cares, and only rarely does anyone notice what he is doing throughout the day as long as the trash cans in patient rooms are emptied, toilet paper throughout the hospital is replenished every night, and the hallways are polished to a mirror finish. Invisibility is one of the powerful tools he learned firsthand as a sniper in Vietnam. And because everyone at the Cooper VA has turned their eyes from the depressing view of the National Cemetery for so long, no one even notices the new garden or the hummingbirds until late April.

Even as he dug the holes and planted the seeds he knew would blossom into homing beacons, he also knew the creation of the garden was more for *her* than for anyone else—and so he wasn't surprised that *she* would be the one to finally discover his creation. Wasn't *she* the reason he was really here, or had he only hoped?

So, here's how Willis's garden creation was finally discovered:

One late-April morning Willis's favorite nurse is checking the morphine drip connected to a terminally ill soldier on her floor when the soldier asks to feel April on his skin.

Phoebe unlocks the window and shoves it outward. Ahead of her lie the buried remains of thousands—Cooper's own and its adopted ones, including her second cousin Alvis, and the boy she kissed as he took his last breath. For some time, though, Phoebe has been pretending not to remember that boy's name. The memory of him conjures the same still-torturous flashbacks she has been avoiding yet carrying all these years of severed legs and arms piled in an enormous trash container in the corner of their Army field medic hospital, and of that particular boy's hand that lies atop the pile of crooked obscenity. *I'm-here-pay-attention-to-me*, the boy's hand seems to say, almost waving as if still attached to that beautiful boy in the bed just a few feet away who will wake soon when the morphine wears off. And when he wakes, he'll scream obscenities at her and demand that she return his arm because *What right did you have to take what wasn't yours?* What right indeed? He'll swear he can still feel the arm, *even the god-forsaken dirt under his fingernails.* She'll remember his dirty fingernails too, because during a second of madness, she nearly pulled the severed brown arm from the pile to dig out the dirt from underneath those beautiful nails because, *It's the least I can do for a mother who cleaned them when this boy was her baby, and whole.*

Later, she will admit to Willis and others that she had pushed open the window of her patient's stale hospital room, willing herself to ignore the depressing vision of the cemetery dead that lay before her, and was overcome by a stirring, brilliant flash of color from below. Forgetting her surroundings for perhaps the first time since she was a combat nurse, she shrieks, "Oh my God, come see this!" (And Willis can easily imagine her *come-see-this* holds the force of a military order. He has seen Phoebe in action. No surprise to him that the terminally ill soldier in the bed behind her would grab both bedside rails in an attempt to comply. Plenty of men in worse shape, including him, have carried out Phoebe's commands: *Breathe, soldier! Stay with me, Marine!*)

According to Phoebe's retelling, an orderly walks in the room with a lunch tray for a soldier too ill to stomach it. "Come here," Phoebe says to the orderly, and waves. "You won't believe this."

The orderly sets down the food tray, she will tell her doctor and Willis later, and joins her at the window. The orderly's eyes widen. "When did that happen?"

Now the dying soldier is determined to see for himself, only he's too weak to sit up, much less swing his puny legs out of bed. "*What?* What is it?"

Phoebe tugs playfully at the orderly's sleeve. "Isn't it beautiful? It's like a Monet—come to life."

"Help me out of this bed," the soldier shouts and rattles both hand rails. Phoebe and the orderly spring to his aid and assist the weak soldier to his feet. They have to nearly carry him to the window. But once he's there... "I'll be damned," he says, and repeats this several times. "Will you look at that."

How long they stand there Phoebe can't recall, or remember what eventually breaks the spell for the three of them—the nurse, the orderly, and the dying soldier—but for a few minutes anyway, three are One, cocooned in a swath of April and the miracle of an impressionistic painting replete with live hummingbirds.

Word spreads quickly throughout the Cooper VA. Soon, caregivers and visitors rediscover the east dining room, especially around three every afternoon when Willis refills the feeders with his sugar water concoction and parks himself on the stone bench between the bird baths to hand feed the tiny, dazzling birds. Children of veterans press their faces and hands against the glass windows. Their musical shrieks of glee and their tiny hand slaps against the glass beckon braver, more curious hummingbirds to zip-zag closer to the adoring onlookers, rewarding the children with aerial feats of hovering—even a little magical backward flying.

Patients in the rooms above Willis shove open their windows, or their visitors or nurses do, to catch a glimpse of him feeding the hummingbirds every afternoon, weather permitting. Of course, not everyone at the VA will be happy about Willis's garden. The head nurse, according to Phoebe, dares to lodge a formal complaint when her staff begins to linger too long on breaks. But nothing official ever reaches Willis, of course.

It's been several weeks now since Phoebe discovered the hummingbird garden and uncloaked Willis as a somebody at the Cooper VA, not that he sought that sort of thing, or that the notoriety lasted long. He is back to being Invisible Willis, except around three every day when he becomes seen as the outstretched hand that feeds the Cooper VA hummingbirds. Willis prefers this power of invisibility. He sees himself as merely a corrector, a solver of problems. *What* problems matter little to him—a leaky or stopped up toilet, a clogged drain… or the depressing view of a cemetery. All problems are the same; some just appear more complex at first.

Take Phoebe's problem—her flashback of that beautiful boy's severed hand waving above the pile of knobby bones tossed in the trash, a haunting flashback that returns over and over. A haunting that Phoebe has tried for decades to ignore. But when she awakes—when we all awake—we discover that this life we've been trying so hard to ignore is the life we've chosen for ourselves since before we were born. For a while, this discovery is even harder to accept—what *we've* chosen to create for ourselves. Many of us will never accept our choices, despite the knowing that lies crystalized within each of us. Why is this so hard to accept? Sometimes Willis forgets how hard it was for him, even now paying homage to the old pattern of life that was intricately and beautifully woven from the fabric of second chances. Pay homage, sure, but the truest gift lies within the allowance of a new elegance of consciousness—one that is, thankfully, edging out the old.

So, Willis is here to help Phoebe prepare for and accept this new elegance. For the past two afternoons, he has been stealing glances toward the barred windows at the top of the north-facing tower and manifesting a wishful prayer for a glimpse of the softly sagging face of his favorite nurse.

Accept your gifts.

But on this particular morning, even thoughts of Phoebe give way to the coming of the boy as Willis pushes his janitorial cart slowly past his military straight rows of tables and chairs. Once he reaches the sickening smell of food and the jarring clamor of porcelain on porcelain, he parks the cart along a side wall near Teana Martin's cash register. Teana is ringing up the breakfast of two doctors and hasn't noticed Willis yet, or she'd be hollering something over a shoulder at him just to spite the two doctors. This is Teana's cafeteria. Here, she's the one in charge.

The boy is coming.

He just can't shake the boy. *In a previous life,* Willis could say to him, already rehearsing a script in his head, *I was a boy, too—mucking through Vietnam with jungle rot and swamp ass—so ain't* nothing *what it seems to be, Boy.*

And just like that, a familiar cosmic wave of sadness threatens Willis's equilibrium. When a widening circle of shock reaches his heart, he steadies himself by holding onto the janitorial cart. Underneath Teana Martin's chirping with two doctors, Willis hears his mind racing to reason with his stubborn heart. "This is too much," Willis whispers against the swell of emotion. He pulls a white handkerchief from a back pocket of his workman trousers. "*Too* much." But the boy is coming.

No, the boy is here.

By the time Willis slides his sparse tray forward, Teana Martin is replacing the spool of receipt paper at the cash register. She glances down at the two biscuits on his tray, both her hands still wrestling with the spool and the machine, and says, "You going to eat my biscuits today, Mr. Willis, or feed 'em to that hawk again?"

"*You* made the biscuits today, Miss Teana? I better have a taste, then—your cooking might accidentally kill that hawk."

Teana Martin leans her head back and howls at the ceiling. "I may not have time for baking biscuits anymore, but I definitely see to it they get baked right." She punches a register button and waits for the register tape to print a test. She uses this moment to lean closer to Willis. They are two conspiratorial allies. Her smile disappears. "How's our favorite nurse today?" she whispers. "You been up there yet?"

On any given weekday at the Cooper VA, more than two thousand caregivers, administrators, and volunteers show up to work—never mind the thousands of patients and their families who move in and about the hospital. As the seventh largest employer in the valley, and with a daily population larger than half the closest towns, the Cooper VA could be considered a small town, in and of itself. And as anyone from a small town will tell you, life in a small town is anything but private—far less so for a VA nurse such as former Army Lieutenant Phoebe Kennedy. At the Cooper VA—*once you crack, you can never go back.*

Willis looks down at the two butter-yellow biscuits on his tray. He is searching for the proper equality of words plus tone. Everything he says will be repeated. Everything within the walls of the Cooper VA is overheard and measured and weighed. "Heading there now."

The cash register is ready for business, and Teana's face lifts back to its usual cheer. "You tell her we're all pulling for her? Got to help knowing so many folks in your corner." She rings up the charge for the biscuits.

"Sure—it's got to help," he says, and fishes a five-dollar bill from a shirt pocket. "Keep the change."

"Oh, no-*no!*" Teana shakes her head and rifles through the cash drawer. She places three singles on Willis's tray, careful to prevent the money from touching his biscuits even if they are for a hawk. "You can't be doing this every morning, Mr. Willis. Either you trying to starve yourself to death or go broke—I can't figure which."

"Isn't the prom this weekend?"

"I wish it was—wish the whole thing was over." Willis knows Teana has been saving since Christmas for what she wishes she'd been saving for since her daughter started high school. Time has gotten away from her. But it wouldn't have mattered, she reasons, because every time she puts a little away, something always breaks and needs fixing. Usually the car. Right now, the tires are so bald she can hydroplane down the mountain to work the next time it rains. She has no idea how she'll drive her daughter over the mountains to college in a few months.

Willis pulls a napkin from the dispenser beside the register and wraps up the two biscuits. He nods at the money left on the tray, and then toward a woman wearing a red VA volunteer blazer who is hurriedly pushing a tray toward them, grabbing items along the way—a banana, a plastic bottle of juice, another plastic bottle of something purple. "I bet *somebody* comes along who could use that." He winks at Teana and walks toward his janitorial cart.

The woman in the red volunteer blazer has paused in front of the coffee machines, possibly undecided between decaf and regular. Teana slides Willis's three singles from his tray and inside the front pocket of her smock. Willis grins and pushes his cart toward the elevator in the hallway. After all, Teana has a daughter to dress for the senior prom in two weeks.

CHAPTER 2

THREE nurses in colorful scrubs—*when did nurses stop wearing white?*—are immersed in conversation when they emerge from the elevator. Not one nods nor speaks to Willis. He pushes the janitorial cart inside the elevator and punches the button. Once inside, Willis dissects the scent of coconut shampoo from antiseptic cleaner, and both of these from the lingering aroma of a stack of breakfast trays that must have been sent up late: bitter coffee, buttered toast, bacon, a hint of cinnamon—no doubt the special request and culprit for the late trays.

The elevator doors open at the sixteenth floor of the north tower and to a hallway. According to directional signage, he can turn right for outpatient or choose left for Phoebe. A left represents the past—his and Phoebe's. He turns left.

The occasional squeak of his cart catches the attention of two women in scrubs at the main desk of the visitor waiting lobby twenty feet ahead of him. The women glance up from their tasks. Seeing nothing or no one of importance, they bury their heads.

Willis parks the cart along a wall near their desk. He grabs three plastic trash can liners and steps in front of the two large closed doors that again require the attention of one of the women. He's not sure who finally notices him and buzzes him through because neither woman looks up nor appears to have moved in his favor. Nonetheless, he hears the loud thud of a released lock. He pushes the metal square button attached to the wall and both doors open to the chaos of shrieks and a stench powerful enough to conjure memories of the pungent open sewers that once flowed throughout Southeast Asia. He knows what this means: Phoebe is trapped somewhere in the past, somewhere in the middle of hell, and it's his job to lead her home.

Willis is alone in the hallway, but not alone. Above him are cameras that attempt to capture everything. He begins a methodical walk toward the large group room on the left. On this floor, anything can become a trigger. Any sound, such as an innocent squeak from one of the wheels on his cart, or any smell such as his cleaning supplies; all reasons why he never pushes the janitorial cart beyond the nurses' station. He's not bothered by all the walking back and forth. Right now, he's here for Phoebe anyway. Tonight, he'll return when the patients are locked in their rooms and he'll empty the trash for real, and wipe down the walls, returning the group room to a blank canvas that's ready to capture the next day's proof of pain.

Ahead of him, two orderlies have emerged from the group room with an unruly veteran-patient between them. The resistance is mild, but the aggravation is apparent. One of the orderlies is twisting the veteran's arm too far behind his back, and the man is howling. Willis doesn't recognize this patient—thick beard, long dark ponytail, mid-thirties perhaps. They get younger and younger. They come and they go. Come and go. Come and never return: *Lost another one.* Some veterans will stay indefinitely—rescued from homeless shelters or park benches. Some rarely speak. Others can't stop talking, or screaming like this bearded fellow, or can't stop trying to scale the walls of the group room, or can't stop finger-painting the walls and floors with their own feces.

The unruly veteran-patient catches a glimpse of Willis, so Willis drops slowly into a crouch and playfully demonstrates a stealthy fox-walk up and down the hallway. The patient stops screaming. His face scrunches in confusion, and then relaxes into recognition. He smiles. Willis smiles.

As the two orderlies escort the now-calm veteran-patient down the hall, the patient looks over his left shoulder, and shouts at Willis, "I see you! I see you!" The double doors at the far end of the hallway swing open like jaws to an abyss, thanks to whoever is watching on camera. The orderlies disappear into the abyss with the veteran between them. But the veteran turns for one last glimpse of Willis, and as the doors begin their path back to closure, Willis hears the veteran laugh out, "I see you!"

Phoebe sits in a chair by the window. The window is barred, of course. The Cooper VA has learned to take no chances. Death is too final here. But if Phoebe were to press her forehead to the window, she could see the garden, ever more impressionistic from this height. Of course, the hummingbirds are likely to appear as crisscrossing lines of confusion.

With her head resting against the back of the chair and her eyes closed, she appears asleep. Not impossible, even with the earsplitting noise bursts at times. Veteran-patients are kept heavily medicated for their own good, or for the good of Cooper VA statistics. Whatever the reason, Willis appreciates the effort even though he knows they have yet to understand what part they're supposed to be fixing. *You can restart a dead car battery with a jump, but you're still not going anywhere when the car's up on blocks.*

He makes his way slowly toward her, careful not to set off a trigger for other patients. She is wearing the issued prison-like clothing—a light gray jumpsuit that when she finally stands to look out the window with him in a few minutes will appear to have swallowed her tiny frame. On her feet are the black slip-ons—another standard issue to every patient on the psych ward. Just before he reaches her, she senses his energy and opens her eyes. Or tries to. The eyes appear to have a mind of their own. But they can't prevent the corners of her mouth from rising or the escaping of, "Hawk, you're here." He tucks the plastic trash can liners inside his trousers and drops to his knees. He covers her icy hands with his. She is drifting in and out. Only the occasional sigh lets him know that his energy steadily warms her. The room has quieted now. Every veteran-patient has become still and content, as if everyone's time-released medication was synchronized.

In a few moments, Phoebe's eyes will flutter open and she will see him again, as if for the first time in a long time. She will slide her hands from under his, straighten herself in the chair, and say, *How long you been here, Hawk?* This is her nickname for him since their first meeting in hell after he had awakened from a nightmare about being under fire and decided he was still dreaming when he discovered an angel hovering above him. She was light—a whirling dervish of sweet-girl-from-back-home and drill sergeant. When he jolted from the nightmare, he heard, "Lie still, Hawk," and she rested one of these very delicate hands, yet heavy and secure as an anchor, on his chest. *Hawk?* Finally, he'd thought, someone in this god-forsaken country who sees him, remembers him for who he truly is, and warm joy had flooded his body and carried him back to the original land of his ancestors, to the mountains surrounding Cooper. As he'd floated closer, they'd opened their arms for him—Father, *Blue Eagle,* killed in the Second Great War, and the man who raised Willis, his grandfather *White Feather.*

But for now in the Cooper VA while Phoebe sleeps in the chair of the psych ward, Willis closes his eyes and dreams. They are back in the land of jungle and blood, the lights are flickering, and overhead is the airborne *thump-whoosh* of mortar after mortar. She leaves his side to comfort a strapped-in, paralyzed soldier. His voice has risen to hysteria above the shuddering of nearby explosions. "They're coming…I can hear them just outside…they're almost here…don't leave me in here alone with them…." Willis disobeys an earlier Phoebe-order and cranes his neck to lock eyes with the soldier—before the lights finally go out.

She is stirring now. Her feather-lashes quiver. *So little time.* He turns over each hand to explore all of her intersecting pathways. A thousand lifetimes—*each journey gifted with the power of save-soothe-steel.*

"How long you been here, Hawk?" she apologizes and slides her hands from under his to straighten herself in the chair. Willis stands. Secures the plastic liners. *One-two-three.* Leave not one behind, or he triggers a frenzy-dive at an appealing solution for those locked in a world void of shoelaces.

The others in the room are stirring too.

The polarity of energy is palpable.

Time for him will soon run out.

The boy is here.

"Hawk—I let you down," she says. "I let everyone down." Her words call forth Shame. Shame never wastes time. Shame is *ready-set-go.* Shame delivered Phoebe to this ward and this chair—the way it will soon deliver the boy to Willis. Shame tints Phoebe's pale neck and face to ruby-throated hummingbird. He has never loved her more.

Shame also causes Phoebe to look away from him, to look out the window where her only view from this chair will be the cemetery of thirty-eight-thousand-*soon-plus-one.* A better view, the garden view he created for her most of all, is but a few feet below. All she has to do is walk to that window and look for it.

Accept your gifts.

"Please go, Hawk. Please don't—"

What she wants to hear from him is an absolution that's not his to extend. He would deny her nothing. *Beyond my paygrade,* he would joke if circumstances were lighter. So he says instead, "Lieutenant Phoebe Kennedy," reaching backward to pull her forward. Lieutenant Phoebe, a light force of healing *back there,* will be an even brighter light force now, if she will allow it. This is Phoebe's problem—everyone's problem. But Willis is not here for everyone. That's just the way it works. Willis is here for Phoebe—and the boy.

He glances around the group room at the undulating sea of gray souls. These souls are not broken, as the outsiders claim. These souls, like Phoebe, have merely forgotten who they really are and why they are here. And every time someone like Willis shows up to remind them, they cover their ears, at first. No one hears the Truth about themselves until they're ready to listen. Even then, when Truth doesn't align with their little truth because Goliath-Guilt covers little truth's ears…these become the souls imprisoned by the darkest remembrances of things past. Phoebe's darkest remembrances have been chasing her since she emerged from the jungles back there. She thought she could outrun the dark remembrance of things past, but Dark never gives up. Dark lies in wait until Shame dims the Light of Worthiness, or snuffs it out. Until Phoebe accepts again that she is still worthy of her role here as a Lightworker, she will be stuck in this gray borderland with the others, with the screamers and feces-painting-artists. He glances around at all the gray soldiers. Phoebe is the only woman, but others are coming. Spirit is spirit. Not man nor woman, nor any other label you think to apply. Label is not the same as name, though. *Don't move, Hawk.*

This time, Willis says loud enough to reach her all the way back there, for that's where she's gone again, "Lieutenant Phoebe Kennedy." And this time, Phoebe sharply turns to face him. There she is, returned—her face a quizzical roadmap that will lead them together out of this hell. He leans over, kisses her damp forehead, and whispers the absolution: "Lieutenant Phoebe—when did you nurses stop wearing white?"

Down the long hallway to the double doors that a watcher is about to open for him, he carries the sound of Phoebe-laughter in his head and heart. And when the doors open, Phoebe-laughter spills into the lobby with him and for some reason, the two women at the lobby desk spring to their feet.

CHAPTER 3

The boy is here.

THE boy arrives on a Thursday, not that the day of the week for the boy's arrival holds any auspicious meaning. At this point, every day feels the same to Willis, except Saturday and Sunday when weekend traffic flows like a steady river of sorrow through the National Cemetery. From a top floor, Willis serves as witness to the synchronicity of heartache. They exit their cars with awkward, gentle efforts. They bring their children and then reprimand them for being childlike. They shuffle toward a grave of someone they are trying not to forget. Once there, they tidy up, replacing the cone-shaped gray-granite urns of dead flowers with fresh ones, or exchange the plastic poinsettias of the previous season for plastic spring daisies, white magnolia blossoms, pink lilies, and ferns. Not everyone leaves flowers. A few will leave behind rolled-up, handwritten notes they shove deep inside the urns.

Willis reads all the notes.

Somebody should, don't you think?

And Willis answers all the notes.

Somebody should, don't you think?

On weekends when one-third of the hospital closes down, he also glides past the locked doors of administrators and doctors. Willis can open any door he wishes. He holds the master key to everything at the Cooper VA.

That's why the previous Sunday afternoon, he let himself inside Dr. Julia Renn's office. He knew the boy was coming soon—but time is irrelevant. Soon could have meant anything. Like the intensifying internal energy a cicada feels just before its transformation, Willis senses the boy's arrival is sooner rather than later. Preparations must be made, and this is why a few days before the boy's arrival, Willis unlocked the door to the suite of offices belonging to Dr. Julia Renn and her staff. He began in the outer office, sitting in a chair the boy was most likely to choose. From this chair, Willis absorbed every detail—the receptionist's desk, and her view of the mountains. The two candy dishes. One held striped peppermints, individually wrapped. The other, an assortment of popular chocolates. Which dish would the boy choose? He closed his eyes for the answer, took a deep breath—*hold-it-hold-it*—and then surrendered. His grandfather had shared the ancient techniques for mind-seeing. *Remote viewing*, they call it today. In the late seventies, the military developed the Stargate Project to harness the power of mind-seeing. The project failed, of course, as do most marriages of incompatible Intention and Design.

So, peppermint or chocolate?

When the answer finally materialized, he shook his head.

The boy is coming.

Willis stood and walked around the outer office, pausing at a magazine rack. Cooking, gardening, and fitness. Nothing of interest to the boy. For the walls, Dr. Renn had chosen abstract landscapes, all void of precise details for a reason. Less sensory aggravation, less triggering mechanism.

No one at the Cooper VA or elsewhere in the world knew how to cure the mind of a man or woman who has seen and experienced what no man or woman should see and experience. In ancient Greece, warriors returning from battle gathered before their communities to share their stories and to pay respect to the fallen. Even then, the Greeks understood the challenge of reintegration for its warriors. They understood how easy it was for ordinary citizens to undermine the depth and breadth of sacrifice that comes with military service, and so the purpose of sharing the warrior's story was two-fold. The warrior emptied the enormous weight still pressing upon his heart and mind. The citizen absorbed the gravity, and extended both gratitude and forgiveness. No one remembers the day Heroism showed up dressed as repressed Martyrdom. Soon, various styles of repressed martyrdom became the fashion of the day.

But after the Great War, veterans with battle fatigue began to stumble toward the Cooper VA. The bravest ones begged for help. Only a few survived the lobotomies. The cemetery acreage had to be expanded. Still, they came—the weary warriors and the desperate, frightened families who dragged in their sons and husbands with *fix-him-or-keep-him* orders.

That's why you had to admire Dr. Julia Renn. As a case worker, she refuses to give up. Sweat lodges, couples retreats, psychotropic drugs, family counseling, electric shock therapy, creative writing workshops, art therapy, modern dance, yoga, meditation, yoga *with* meditation, drumming, and Willis's favorite—singing bowls flown in from Tibet to help reset calibrations on the car-battery-brain.

But her patients scream obscenities at her, or call her a kook, or throw the bowl lovingly crafted by Tibetan monks from ancient rituals with materials of the highest-most-sacred-healing-vibrations on Earth across the room, or threaten to quit and do for a while and return, or silently threaten to kill her after she shines light on a corner they prefer to keep dark. They lodge formal complaints. They demand her dismissal. Dr. Renn is unflappable. What she doesn't want to accept is that you can't force Atonement down the throat of self-flagellation, not even down a screaming-hungry baby bird throat if the baby bird won't stop screaming long enough to swallow what's good for it.

But Dr. Renn offers.

And offers.

And offers.

That Sunday afternoon, Willis also unlocked Dr. Renn's office and seeing it decorated as the outer one, he sat in her chair for a while, facing the three chairs across the desk. He tried to picture the boy and his parents walking in, and Dr. Renn gesturing toward the three chairs. The parents will expect the boy to take the middle, though he'll resist. He'll turn his back on them and fall into the corner of the sofa against the other wall, and sling a leg onto the sofa. His expensive running shoe will hang off the side. He knows better than to put a shoe on any sofa. But then his father will speak to him in a baritone hush the boy will recognize as that moment before the lid blows from the proverbial pot, releasing *Charlie*. The boy will sit up straight. Not even this boy wants responsibility for unleashing *Charlie*. The mother, little song-stolen canary, will glance from boy to husband to Dr. Renn—*help-help, help-help*. The boy will jump to his feet and make the mistake of yanking the middle chair backward for what he expects his father to buy as the boy's necessary and personal real estate.

Dr. Renn will have to step in, "Colonel Condor—."

Disarmed, Colonel Christopher Condor, Air Force B-52 bomber pilot responsible for at least two thousand deaths of noncombatants in Iraq during Desert Storm, will place *Charlie* at ease, and take a seat.

The boy will sulk. He will offer nothing beyond *I-don't-knows* and shrugs. Eventually, he will sense an exit strategy, perhaps the way Willis senses the need to prepare for the boy's arrival.

A cicada is the only insect that also chooses its birthdate.

Instead of a left to use the facilities, the boy will take a right.

The boy is coming.

Four days later.

On *that* Thursday and lunch time, Teana Martin leaves her cash register and a line of customers when she sees Willis walking toward the cafeteria's exit door. "Mr. Willis, where you been?" The last time Willis saw Teana Martin this flustered she was standing in water above her ankles after a kitchen pipe burst. "You the only one in this hospital without a phone," she says. So, Willis turns for the kitchen until Teana grabs the sleeve of his arm, nearly causing him to drop the two biscuits he's still got wrapped in a napkin. "Where you going? You got to get outside. I done called

security, but probably too late by the time they get here."
She nods toward the cemetery, and that's when Willis sees
the hawk flying toward the top of a tree above the stone-
columned entrance. Following the hawk is a rock that's
been launched with force from unseen weaponry. And then
another rock—this one so close the hawk flies to a higher
branch. "I can't do everything around here," she says and
pushes Willis toward the door. "Hurry up before he kills that
hawk!" Another rock soars overhead toward the hawk.

The hawk refuses to leave.

The hawk is waiting for Willis.

But the hawk isn't the only one.

The boy is here.

Willis is holding tight the biscuits and his tongue. Another
rock like a launched mortar round flies overhead. When
Willis rounds the red-bricked corner of the north wall, he
sees the boy. *Cut from the cloth of the father.* And the boy sees
Willis, and drops a handful of rocks onto the gravel pile in the
wheelbarrow that Willis will be pushing later this afternoon
to the sewer retention pond. The boy wipes gravel dust from
his hands. His jeans hold the evidence of two hand prints, and
as Willis marches closer, the boy runs to the back door that
leads to a stairwell used in case of fire. "Wait right there, *boy!*"
Willis shouts. The boy disobeys and yanks the door handle
with such force that when the door refuses to open, the boy
falls to the ground. Quickly, he's back to his feet. He grabs
the handle again, because he can't yet grasp that the entrance
to a door he opened from the inside a few moments ago
requires a key and that he is trapped outside with a mad man
on approach.

As Willis gets closer, he pulls forward a fat ring of keys that are attached to his belt. "Security," he says. "All outside doors are locked. Lucky for us I got a key for this door somewhere on this ring."

The boy reeks of fear-sweat. But he's just a boy. Fourteen, tops. He has the same mop-looking haircut as most boys his age. This is the time in a boy's life when he can't bear not to fit in. The rest of his life he'll spend searching for ways to stand out. He's wearing baggy jeans, a wrinkled collared shirt his mom probably insisted he wear so he pulled it last minute from the bottom of an unfolded pile of laundry, and the expensive athletic shoes most boys his age are wearing.

Finally, Willis comes face-to-face with the boy.

At the door, Willis tries several keys and fails. He sighs and feigns frustration and mutters about why nobody's ever bothered to color code all these keys with each outside door. Then, "You got somewhere to be right this second?" The boy, like most kids his age, just shrugs. "Does that mean yes or no?"

"Guess not."

"Then we got some making up to do with a hawk." The boy has been growing twitchier with every second, and Willis suspects the boy might even make a run for it. "You had time to throw rocks at that hawk, didn't you?" As Willis heads down the hill, he pauses to look over a shoulder at the boy. The boy is frozen in place; he is staring east and down at the cemetery with its rows and rows and rows of small white headstones. Willis shouts back up the hill. "Everything's already dead down *there*—you come with me."

The boy shrugs.

Relents.

Willis leads the boy to a round picnic table in the shade of a well-manicured magnolia tree that stands defiant in the middle of a long line of junipers and cypresses and long-leaf pines. The magnolia blossoms have released their fragrance, and Willis can't think of a more heavenly fragrance on this earth unless it's the fragrance combination of gardenia and roses, a scent forever linking him to Phoebe. But right now, his thoughts must remain focused on the boy. The boy is standing behind one of the curved benches. "You waiting on an order to sit?" The boy looks embarrassed and climbs over the bench. He watches Willis unwrap the two biscuits. The biscuits have turned from butter-yellow to withered-dry, but the hawk won't care. The hawk will be grateful. "Now you be real still and watch first." Willis is waiting for a response. The boy shrugs. "You got a name?" Willis says, and the boy shrugs. "You been out here trying to kill my hawk—least you owe me is a name."

"I wasn't throwing rocks at the hawk," the boy says, and brushes the white-blond mop out of his eyes. "I was just trying to hit that tree over there," and points to the tree near the cemetery entrance, the one the hawk had flown to for safety during the rock attack.

Willis tears apart the first biscuit and shapes the crumbs into a small tower. The boy watches. Willis senses the boy's curiosity, and the desire to help. The boy knows he's being watched and refuses to look away from the shredding process and the growing pile of bread crumbs. When the boy can stand it no longer, he blurts, "What happened to your hand?"

"Which one?" Willis teases, and the boy squirms. Willis knows the boy's been taught not to ask such questions, especially at the Cooper VA. And herein lies the problem.

Willis senses now what is required of him. The boy is a Knower. He's here to seek Knowledge as pure and clear as the divine crystal embedded within him, and then to share what he knows with the world at the right time. Everyone has a purpose. Knowing, like other purposes, lies in wait for the perfect soupy sludge of circumstances to congeal. Knowing has chosen this boy. Or the boy has chosen Knowing—not even Willis has all the answers. The boy innately knows that Willis holds a key to the living library. Willis innately knows this boy must ask the hard questions, even all the ones he's been taught not to ask. Like not staring at the amputees rolling through the Cooper VA hospital when this boy longs to hear, needs to hear, the details of every story. And who says the amputees aren't begging to be asked and heard? So, it's the boy's intention that needs correction. Willis sees this now. From their stories the boy would weave another, because if he hears enough stories, asks enough questions, *Were you in Iraq?* for example, he believes he can justify the hatred for his father's decorated war actions, and lay proof at the feet, or wheelchair, of a less-than-whole person. He's hoping Willis will be the One.

Because the boy's youth still senses time as more conceptual than linear, Willis appears ageless, young enough to play the role of victim for the story of this boy and the father he so desperately longs to hate. Of course, none of this is yet a conscious thought to the boy. Or to his parents. Or even to Cooper's expert, Dr. Julia Renn. That's why the boy's here. To unlearn his way back to Knowing. But the unlearning will take time. Hate—like Shame, like Dark—comes when called.

Willis attacks the second biscuit with the black steel hook that is his left hand and starts the shredding process. The boy's been taught to look anywhere at a man or woman but at what's missing. And here's Willis, shredding biscuits for a hawk, and the boy has no choice but to stare at what's missing, or at its artificial replacement.

Willis has allowed the boy's question to linger in the air with the magnolia fragrance. So, the boy asks another. "Is he really going to eat those? I thought hawks only ate other birds."

"Yeah? What else you know about hawks?" Willis scoops up fallen crumbs. Stalling. When the boy shrugs, Willis says, "Do you know what kind of hawk that is?" The boy shakes his head. Finished, Willis says, "Slide around to the other side of the table—and remember, you stay still when he comes…*if* he comes."

The boy untangles himself from the picnic bench and heads counter-clockwise until Willis takes a step to block him. "Clockwise," he says. He waits for the word and its definition to catch up with the boy.

"Huh?"

"Always walk clockwise," Willis says. What he understands about the power of directions—how walking toward one direction empowers and walking toward the other disempowers—is too much to share with the boy in this moment. This moment is reserved for another lesson.

The boy sweeps aside the mop-hair from his eyes, shrugs, and performs an about face. After they complete the half-dozen steps to reach the opposite side of the table, Willis says, "If you haven't run him off for good, you're about to see something special. But you don't got to share it with everybody, if you know what I mean."

He smiles down at the boy who hesitates but says, "OK, sure."

Willis produces a few clucking and clicking sounds. Nothing. He whispers, "You done it now. Never seen that bird miss a meal. If he don't come when I do *this*, we lost him for good." The boy looks down at the ground to hide his embarrassment. Willis makes a few more clucking and clicking sounds, and follows all this show with a single high-pitched whale of a whistle that causes a dog from somewhere over a hill past the cemetery to bark.

A heavy flap of wings and rustle of feathers from behind them startles the boy, and Willis grabs hold of the boy's shirt sleeve. "Don't move—that bird would just as soon bite off one of your fingers as settle for that pile of crumbs."

The hawk doesn't land on its first approach. Cautious, the hawk glides by and creates a wide circle. The boy's head has turned skyward to follow the hawk, and now that the hawk is behind them again, the boy is turning to follow. Willis grabs the boy's arm this time. "Don't you flinch now—he's got to get close enough to smell you first, and right now you're as ripe as road kill."

But the boy can't help himself. When he senses the hawk is close, he instinctively ducks, covering his head with both hands. "Boy, you don't hear real good, do you? Lucky he didn't snatch a thumb on the way by you." The hawk again passes up the bread tower and lights on the branch of the magnolia. "See? You spooked him."

Willis clucks and clicks softly at the bird. A few seconds later, the hawk leaves the magnolia branch and, making another wide circle, attempts a third approach. This time the boy stands at rigid attention and the hawk lands on the opposite end of the picnic table near the bread tower. The bird cocks its head at the two of them, and hops on yellow-stilt legs toward the small mountain of bread crumbs. When the boy begins to quiver from excitement, Willis places his right hand on the boy's shoulder to steady him.

It doesn't take long for the hawk to whittle down the bread tower. When the bird flies off, the boy, who has been holding his breath as if under water, finally exhales and explodes with, "Wow, that was awesome. How did you train him to do that?"

"Who says the hawk didn't train me?"

Nothing is ever as it seems.

The boy's face holds so much joy and wonder that Willis wonders if he's been wrong about what he has sensed to come. He wants to be wrong. Needs to be wrong about this one.

But nothing is ever as it seems.

Down the hill, a golf cart has emerged between the stone columns of the cemetery entrance. They can hear the sputter of the security guard's walkie-talkie and the hum of the diesel-powered engine. The security guard sees them now, too, and directs the golf cart their way. "Oh, shit!" the boy says, and glances around for escape routes.

Willis says, "A man has to learn when to run and when to be still." He places his hand again on the boy's shoulder. This time the boy tenses and moves away.

As the security guard draws near, he shouts above the diesel rumble, "You Eli Condor?"

"Yeah," the boy says, and self-corrects. "Yes, sir."

The security guard brings the noisy golf cart to a halt. The newborn silence is too-soon interrupted with radio chatter about the missing boy's recovery. The security guard wears a white shirt with a badge, and says, "Your parents are looking for you, son. Your dad's pretty upset. Better hop in and let me drive you around to the front where they're waiting. Sooner you get there the better." The security guard pays no attention to Willis. Nobody notices Willis, except at three in the afternoon.

For the boy, the magic of the hawk has disappeared. So has Willis. The boy slides onto the seat beside the security guard and drops his head and shoulders. The boy does not want to face *Charlie*.

Who would?

CHAPTER 4

BEFORE they faced combat together in Korea, two Marine veterans—Dove Jennings from North Carolina and Harold Jay from West Virginia—met in boot camp. Because Parris Island recruits are alphabetically assigned sleeping racks, Harold Jay slept above Dove Jennings for twelve arduous weeks. They stood rifle inspections side-by-side. Footlocker inspections. Hygiene inspections. They compared spit-shines, and while sitting on their footlockers to spit-shine boots every night before lights out, they quizzed each other on the eleven general orders, or they shared the news from home that arrived that day during mail call. Both men were sweet on girls they planned to marry after Parris Island, because Korea was likely, and Korea was also likely the reason their drill instructors were so hard on them. What was an occasional rifle butt to the back of the head or gut compared to the real thing?

Three times a day during boot camp, Dove Jennings and Harold Jay marched to the chow hall with their platoon. During the few precious minutes allowed for each meal, they wolfed down what they could. During the hours of drill practice or runs in formation, Dove Jennings marched or ran behind Harold Jay in the second squad of their platoon. At the end of twelve weeks, Dove Jennings knew as much about the back of Harold Jay's head, neck, and shoulders as he knew about the back of his own hand.

After a brief graduation ceremony, they boarded a Parris Island bus that carried them to the train station. They rode the same train, filling the time with small talk about looking forward to home cooking and getting married before shipping off for training, until Dove's stop near Raleigh. Dove had orders for radio school. Jay, basic infantry. If either man ever imagined that he'd meet the other again, neither mentioned it. At the train station near Raleigh, Dove hoisted his olive-green sea bag over a shoulder, tucked the brown, official envelope containing his orders for radio school under an arm, and shook the hand of a man he'd come to regard as a brother. Harold Jay would say later that as the train pulled away from Raleigh and chugged toward Parkersburg, West Virginia, the sudden severing of ties with Dove Jennings felt shocking and explosive, as if Jay had just lost a limb.

Both men married their sweethearts and ten days later, reported to training. Two months later, both men kissed their newlywed brides goodbye and headed to California to join up with the Marine division that was soon shipping overseas to Korea. At Camp Pendleton's receiving office, Dove Jennings was standing in line with other Marines and listening to the nervous small talk about first impressions of the Pacific Ocean and the California brown hills surrounding the camp when he noticed something familiar about the Marine who was several ahead of him. "I would have known the back of that head anywhere," he would later joke. Dove called out, "Jay!" Several Marines swiveled to see what they were missing, but not the Marine he was hoping. "Still," he'll tell others for many, many years, "I knew that head like the back of my hand, so next time I holler, 'Hey, *Jay*-bird!'" And that time, the head turned.

Soon both men were deposited by bus to the headquarters of the 5th Marine Regiment, and two weeks later, both men were on a ship with twelve hundred others, bound for Korea. This was the first time either man had been at sea, and life was cramped but not all unpleasant as they anticipated seeing Hawaii for the first time. But after Hawaii, a blanket of unsettlement began to descend upon the ship. As the seas grew choppier and grayer under winter skies, each man wrestled with something like self-doubt. Each carried in his head the stories of those he knew who survived Normandy and Iwo Jima, and of those he knew who didn't. On their ship was a platoon first sergeant, Franks, but they called him Big Red Franks behind his back because his face and neck always looked sunburned. Big Red Franks received the Silver Star from his actions in Iwo, and Dove, Jay, and their fellow Marines stole glances at him as if his aura were too dangerous for lengthy star-gazing. During innermost contemplation, they asked themselves, *Will I be worthy? What will be* my *story?*

To keep every man too exhausted for much contemplation, war-seasoned platoon first sergeants like Big Red Franks kept their men physically occupied with drills of one sort or another, ship deck fitness routines, and rifle cleaning. They ordered their men to clean their rifles every day to prevent salt air contamination, but Dove and Jay suspected the constant rifle cleaning was just another way of giving each Marine something to do with his hands and his time and his mind.

During snatches of free time, the two men wrote letters home that they knew couldn't be mailed until they reached port in Korea. Following Jay's lead, Dove also numbered the outside of his envelopes for his wife, Sarah. The letters were filled with mind-numbing details about boredom at sea and what they had for chow. The letters were often laced with sweet recollections about early dates, silly moments, or about how the women appeared in their dreams the night before. When the ship finally reached port, Dove Jennings and Harold Jay, both assigned to 3rd platoon, 1st battalion, 5th Marines, stood on deck with their platoon and listened for their names during the first mail call. All around them, letters were being ripped open. The air filled with laughter and cheers about babies. One Marine announced the arrival of his devil-pup-son. Another shared the news about his wife giving birth to a *girl,* and he took good-natured ribbing about how he better start honing his rifle skills by shooting *chinks* and *gooks.*

Dove Jennings and Harold Jay also tore into their envelopes. They read each letter with a hunger they didn't realize had been gnawing at them. And when they discovered the news—simultaneously, as they later retell this story over and over at the Cooper VA—they whooped and cheered on the deck of a ship at Inchon in Korea where weeks earlier, the Marines before them had launched a surprise beach landing invasion that quickly brought about the surrender of North Koreans who had crossed the 38th parallel to occupy Inchon. But there, in a strange land where they were expected to halt communist oppression, they discovered the life-changing news that both wives were pregnant. Dove patted Jay on the back and Jay promised to buy Dove the first round at the first bar they'd find during their first shore leave.

But that drink would have to wait. It was October 1950 and time to head ashore. As they exited starboard, both men noticed the convoy of U.S. military trucks and vehicles with Red Cross emblems lined up at the ship's port side, and the long, wavy sea of stretchers headed up the gangplank.

What happens over the next handful of months for the 5th and 7th Marine Regiments at the battle of Pusan, and later at the Chosin Reservoir, is well-documented. MacArthur and others will gravely miscalculate North Korea's threat to call on the Chinese if UN forces cross the 38th parallel and the strength in numbers China will send. The 9th Army will suffer devastating losses. When an Army officer receives a Silver Star on the battlefield by a general who flies in for show to pin the medal and flies out quickly before the fighting resumes, the disgusted 9th Army officer will rip the medal from his chest in front of his troops and toss the medal into the snow.

The Air Force will be ridiculed by the other service branches for its lack of participation.

But the Inchon invasion, battle for Pusan, fighting at the Chosin Reservoir, and the withdrawal that ultimately decimates seven Chinese regiments will fortify Marine Corps legend. Not that the names of Dove Jennings and Harold Jay will be found in history books, but they should be. After the victorious battle at Pusan, they will march on to the Chosin Reservoir, and will be there during the three-day, three-night siege that begins November 27th.

In below-freezing temperatures that first night, Marines at Chosin couldn't dig foxholes; they had to use explosives to crack open the frozen earth. They hadn't even completely set up their base camp before the first attack. The Chinese swarmed over the hills during the night and lobbed grenades. Marines in bare feet and freezing conditions launched mortar attacks, manned machine guns, and fought hand-to-hand when overrun.

The embedded journalists panicked and swarmed Colonel Puller's operations tent. "We've been looking for the enemy for several days now," Colonel Chesty Puller will tell them. "We've finally found them. We're surrounded. That simplifies our problem of finding these people and killing them." But a frightened officer will later ask the colonel for his retreat plan. The officer will be lucky the old man doesn't pull out his pistol and shoot the man dead right there.

Dove, as a radio operator, was supporting artillery when that familiar Chesty voice crackled through his headset with an order for the base artillery commander: "You are ordered to fire on any Marine who abandons his position."

In early December, Marines were ordered to abandon the Chosin Reservoir and to open an escape route to Hungnam port. Dove Jennings and Harold Jay hadn't seen each other since the three-night hell. Each man was torn between two jobs, as it was: defending the Marine next to him and surviving for their wives and their unborn. When a reporter for *Life*, tagging behind Dove, had asked what he wanted for Christmas since MacArthur had publicly promised all American troops would be home for the holidays, a cold-

and-battle-weary Dove turned to the reporter and said, "Give me tomorrow." This quote and a photo of Dove no one, including Sarah, will ever recognize as him ended up on the next cover of *Life*.

To reach the port, Marines had to battle their way down a road fifteen-feet wide through the high Taebak mountain pass with their wounded and dead and every piece of equipment they could keep operational. They fought against brutally frigid conditions, the coldest winter in a hundred and fifty years of North Korean history. They had to keep engines running or they'd freeze. Hot chow froze, too, before a Marine could eat it, and that's saying something since everyone knows how fast a Marine can wolf down his chow.

The Chinese, hiding among rocky cliffs, ambushed the Marines with surprise grenade attacks. When a grenade fell close to Harold Jay and began to roll toward his platoon first sergeant, Big Red Franks, the one who just five years earlier received that Silver Star for heroism during the battle of Iwo Jima, Jay shouted, "Grenade," and hurled his body toward the grenade in an effort to shield his platoon sergeant. The explosion burst Jay's right eardrum. When he opened his eyes, two Marines were looking down on him, talking, but he couldn't make out the words. *Was this death?* He no longer felt cold.

But the two Marines hoisted him to his feet, and the cold returned. That's when Jay saw others attending to what was left of Big Red Franks, who had shoved Jay from the blast in that final tenth of a second before the explosion, absorbing the grenade blast for them all, but especially for Private Harold Jay. Big Red Franks, *Marine most likely now to earn a Medal of Honor*, was still alive, but when Jay discovered Big

Red's legs eerily standing upright together in the deep snow clear on the other side of the pass, he collapsed and wept. *Those should be my legs,* he kept telling himself.

Though Dove Jennings and Harold Jay report they never saw each other after the battle for Pusan, they each had a sense that the other man was still alive. Despite the carnage around them, and the men suffering from a form of blindness called combat hysteria—*Who knew the mind had the power to shut off what it cannot bear to witness?*—Dove, who was providing radio support for the artillery commander in the rear, said he just knew that Jay would be on the other side of this hell, waiting for him. Jay knew that Dove, as a radio operator, had a below-average survival chance because the Chinese wouldn't miss many opportunities to destroy communications, especially communications that received calls for artillery support, but Jay also felt that if any radio operator could survive this, Dove could.

It took thirteen days for the Marines to reach the port—the men putting to good use all their training as basic riflemen first. They fought for every foot of that seventy-eight mile retreat-non-retreat to the port, and left behind them the remains of seven Chinese divisions. Dove would leave behind two toes and a finger to frostbite. What Jay would leave behind wasn't as easily quantified as three missing digits, but no less a sacrifice.

Colonel Chesty Puller would receive his fifth Navy Cross—this one for holding the Chosin Reservoir and for getting his Marines to the port while also decimating more than one hundred thousand Chinese insurgents. He would have a son soon after who would grow into his father's Marine Corps boots, so to speak, and Junior would serve in Vietnam, win a Pulitzer Prize for a biography about being the son of Chesty Puller, and then Junior would shoot himself dead—like so many others.

From their short time in Korea, Dove Jennings and Harold Jay would receive a lifetime of memories—some good, many not-so-good—and a few medals of their own for valor, although the details surrounding the moments of valor they kept between them. They felt the real honor belonged to all those thousands of Marines who didn't make it home to their newborn sons and daughters.

Back home in the mountains of West Virginia with his wife and daughter, Harold Jay's new civilian life pinched like a pair of too-small dress shoes. No matter how hard he tried to stretch or forget or simply accommodate, he couldn't forget the pinch. Nothing about his life felt exactly right. Not his job at the downtown hardware store. Not the evening stretches of time spent with his wife, Becky, and daughter that required him to act opposite of how he felt. What did he feel, exactly? Sadness? An emptiness? He wasn't even sure himself.

And his once beloved West Virginia mountains and brutal winters of his upbringing were now just harsh reminders of Chosin Reservoir and the wave after wave of Chinese insurgency and ambushes through the mountain passes that he and his fellow Marines cleared on the way to the port. Driving around the bend of a mountain on the way to work in the morning or on his way home every evening would cause him to tense behind the wheel. His eyes would leave the road too long in searches above, ahead, and even below every crook and bend for the pop-up of a Chinese attack. When he nearly ran off the road by over-compensating for a curve and heard Becky's scream and the baby's cry, he reached out to Dove who was still living in North Carolina. Dove sympathized and encouraged Jay to move south. The only problem was that Dove and his wife and kids had moved from Raleigh toward the mountains and the winter-cold and the too-similar memories of the Chosin Frozen. Dove's move had been for a job. A man with a limp and half a hand has to take what he can get, he told Jay, even though the Carolina winters aggravated his frostbite injuries.

Jay promised to think about it.

And he did, for one night. When he couldn't sleep, he walked the house, chain-smoking, while his wife and baby slept soundly down the hall. The next morning, he made a few calls to sever ties with his employer and to offer a few explanations to family about why he had to leave. Becky tearfully packed suitcases. Jay could hear her sobs from the bedroom, and pangs of guilt stabbed him. Still, he knew he had to get out of West Virginia before he accidentally killed them with his reckless driving. Something told him that if he lived near Dove—the only person he had ever *really* known in his life and who was the only person who really knew him too—he could survive anything, even brutally cold winters in the mountains of North Carolina. What Jay had finally admitted to himself during that nightlong-chain-smoking-walkabout was that he was in danger, serious danger of harming himself and others. He wasn't fit enough to be the dependable support system his wife and daughter deserved when he was the one who most needed a dependable support system. He didn't know what that would look like. He just knew it would start with his old friend Dove, and that their wives would fast become best friends—the children too. Two days later, Jay and his family left packing instructions for their furniture and his wife's precious family china and drove south to Cooper, North Carolina. They rented the small ranch house down the street from Dove that came up for rent just as Harold Jay and his family were cautiously winding their way down the steep, treacherous West Virginia mountains.

And that's the story of how Dove Jennings and Harold Jay met and ended up in Cooper. But it's what happens next that matters most to Willis and everyone else at the Cooper VA. You see, years later, Dove becomes ill—further complications from those frostbite injuries. Both men are retired by this point, so it's not surprising a health situation will arise for one or both of them. But in Dove's case, his health claims at the Cooper VA will be denied over and over. Dove's health will suffer, and Jay will become so outraged, and terrified of being left alone, that he spends his days and nights unraveling the paperwork bureaucracy of the broken Cooper VA system. When it comes to helping his friend Dove, nothing is too much of a challenge, not to a man who tried to jump on a grenade to save his platoon sergeant and who fought valiantly with India Company, 3/5, through the frozen Taebaek mountain passes of Korea with a Chesty Puller boot up his ass every step of the way.

No Marine quits.

And nothing happens by accident.

So Jay navigates all that red tape, and eventually Dove receives the health care he needs, and certainly deserves. Maybe everyone else in Cooper, North Carolina, and elsewhere has forgotten the Forgotten War, but Dove and Jay and thousands of other Marines and soldiers of the

VFW haven't, and never will. That's what happens when the worst of humanity seeps under your skin—no amount of scrubbing will ever fully remove the stink. But the biggest stink to Dove Jennings and Harold Jay is how poorly the young veterans of today's wars are being treated. Most of them are too shell-shocked still—whether from war trauma or from a rocky re-entry to civilian status. Who has the patience to complete the miles and miles of paperwork after war? So, every weekday at 9:00 a.m., Dove and Jay show up at the Cooper VA and set up shop, so to speak. And whenever a veteran with the look of self-inflicted distress crosses Willis's path, Willis magically and mysteriously ensures the veteran's path crosses Dove's and Jay's. Sometimes this requires a little more planning from Willis for the proper execution.

For example—two weeks before the boy's first arrival….

Dove Jennings and Harold Jay are walking toward the Cooper VA auditorium to join others for the exciting launch of a poetry book written by ninety-six-year-old George Plover. George is a survivor of the Battle of the Bulge, and life in general. You see, George and his wife Sonja lost their only child, George Jr., in Vietnam. Then Sonja dropped dead from a brain aneurysm the day before her seventy-fifth birthday. But when their grandson George III, an Army major stationed in Germany after two tours in Iraq, took his life—a suicide-by-train on the tracks outside Ramstein—George had been personally escorted by Dove and Jay to Dr. Julia Renn's office. Soon after, George was sitting in a one-time, VA-sponsored creative writing workshop. You had to admire Dr. Renn. She could squeeze a budget until it finally spit forth enough blood to create new life, or save one. This time she'd squeezed hard enough to hire an Iraq-war veteran for three months—a woman who had used her G.I. Bill for a master's program in writing and who had published two books already. Fast forward three months and they're all heading by foot or wheelchairs to the auditorium to celebrate George's self-published book of war poetry about the Battle of the Bulge.

Question: Why do you suppose some people like George, who lose far more than most, still find ways to shape and form Chaos, Loss, and Grief into art?

This is what baffles the so-called experts. This is also what inspires a few, such as Dr. Renn and her colleagues. George, the anomaly, has become the Cooper VA hope for a cure. George, the lab rat, lets them draw his blood and run multiple scans on his brain. Dr. Renn and her colleagues compare the scans of George's brain to the brains of the still-suffering. Sadly, they can draw no conclusions other than George's ninety-six-year-old brain appears healthier than the brains of veterans less than half his age.

Because all your issues show up in your tissues.

But this will give Dr. Renn a new idea. What if the Cooper VA were to collect the brain images of its veteran-patients who claim relief through their prescribed psychotropic cocktails, and then use those brain images to build a national database for comparison? The objective—match up veterans with similar brain imaging with those on psychotropic cocktails, and then prescribe the same working psychotropic cocktail. It could work, right? Dr. Renn squeezes the budget for more blood money. She handpicks her research team from around the country—all recognized leaders in their fields: a neuroscientist, neurosurgeon, geneticist, biologist, and a psychologist.

Of course, Willis knows this won't work either. They're still trying to heal the brain when it's the mind and heart that beg for healing. Isn't this why he's here? For Phoebe and for the boy?

We are so much more than we think we are.

Back to George Plover and his poetry celebration in the Cooper VA auditorium—George turned ninety-six a few weeks earlier and probably doesn't weigh ninety-six pounds, yet he's never appeared in public wearing the same thing twice. Every day, a different suit impeccably tailored. George loves color, and for his poetry book launch, he's wearing a maroon sport coat with a shirt the color of a Tahitian sunset. In his lapel is a large tropical-looking flower of some sort with baby's breath and greenery. "Jesus," Dove mumbles toward Jay as George steps up to the microphone for his reading, "is he going to the prom after this?" And Jay chuckles.

George opens with a powerfully sentimental poem about the battle. Nothing rhymes, but thanks to George, Dove and Jay have learned that not all poetry has to rhyme. They're still straining to follow along, leaning toward a meter that doesn't exist, when they hear the ruckus in the hallway.

What do you imagine happens among a group of foreign-war heroes when they hear explosive sounds in the hallway? Those in wheelchairs start issuing orders. The youngest veterans not in wheelchairs have already hit the carpeted deck between the rows of auditorium seating.

But Dove Jennings and Harold Jay?

Dove and Jay are scrambling up the slope of the auditorium *toward* the ruckus. Even before they reach the double doors that will lead them to hurricane-strength Guilt on the other side of the doors, they hear, "You don't want me to go *Charlie* on you! Don't make me go *Charlie* on you!"

What Dove and Jay can't see yet is that on the other side of the auditorium doors, a category-five hurricane is whirling toward them, toward Willis, and toward the exit door near the auditorium. Willis needs to stall this hurricane force of Guilt to give Dove and Jay more time—they're older now, you see, and Dove has that limp that's demanding a hip replacement. So, Willis's timing has to be perfect. And it is. At just the exact moment, Willis gives that old janitorial cart with the squeaky-loose wheel a sacrificial shove. The cart goes flying off, and just before crossing the path of the oncoming hurricane, the cart even wobbles side-to-side on two wheels until the magical blending of physics and gravity upends Willis's entire janitorial operation. Imagine the cart-crash of metal against Willis's highly polished floors and the sudden airborne release of cleaners, all those brushes, even the two Teana Martin biscuits he'd bought for the hawk that morning. Here come Dove and Jay now, bursting from the auditorium and landing smack in the middle of the eerily calm eye of Hurricane *Charlie* while at their feet lies the cart and strewn supplies—what they obviously assume as *Charlie* storm damage.

And here comes Dr. Julia Renn who was front-row-center for George's poetry reading. The doctor steps over brushes and cleaning supplies and attempts to catch her breath, right hand over her heart. She picks her spot in the hallway and stands quietly nearby while Dove Jennings and Harold Jay work *their* magic. Not everyone around the Cooper VA is as appreciative of the influence wielded by Dove and Jay as Dr. Renn and Willis.

Charlie, attempting to reorganize to destructive Hurricane Guilt energy, stands in the center of the hallway, looking at the janitorial mess in his way, and shouts, "Nobody gives a flying fuck about what I'm doing over there." *Charlie* paces up and down and flaps his arms. "I'm following orders and back here, nobody gives a fuck—they're eating their fucking McDonald's and streaming fucking videos like nothing in the world has changed while I'm carpet bombing Baghdad all the way back to fucking Babylon...."

Dove and Jay nod and nod and nod. Dove, arms folded across his chest, stands slightly crooked because of that bad hip. Jay's hands rest on his hips. This is not their first category-5 hurricane. They have weathered too many, including their own. They know to wait for the winds of Hurricane *Charlie* to blow through and over and around them until the winds finally drop to tropical storm status. This will be when Dove and Jay speak for the first time.

When *Charlie* finally descends to that tropical storm status, Dove and Jay see their opening. They begin by validating all the disappointment that fueled the buildup to Hurricane *Charlie*. And then they share well-choreographed details about their time in Korea and about their own rocky homecomings. They talk about burying Dove's son, Steven Lee, twenty years after the boy's return from Vietnam, and how Dove had wanted to crawl down in that hole with his son. So had Sarah and their daughter, Mary-Linda. But so had Jay who had loved the boy as his own. Even Jay and Becky's daughter, Lori Elizabeth, had flown in from California to attend the funeral of the boy she'd loved her whole life as a brother. After mourners began to disperse that day for their cars, the boy's parents, sister,

Jay, his wife, and their daughter, clung hand-in-hand to one another at the edge of Steven Lee's grave and unleashed a rain of Sorrow and Regret into that deep abyss.

Dove nods east, toward the cemetery. His voice is warbling with emotion. "Every day—don't you know I wish I could trade places with him."

Then Jay mentions George Plover's grandson, the Army major who parked his car on a railroad track in Germany, and left behind a loving wife, Yvonne, and a beautiful daughter, Victoria, who would forever carry the pangs of Abandonment. And despite Dr. Renn's nearby presence—because the mission always comes first or because both men resent that Dr. Renn won't authorize them visitation with their favorite Cooper VA nurse—both Dove and Jay lob in a few hurricane-force *fucks* for special effects.

"You've come to the right place," Dove says. "Congratulate yourself for taking this step."

Harold Jay finally waves over Dr. Renn. "You won't find a better veterans-advocate." He means it too. He's probably thinking about what Dove told him earlier, about how the doctor convinced Dove that a June-gloom was normal since it was June a year ago that Dove's son Steven Lee ended his life. Dove had been thinking lately of ending his too. But that June-gloom afternoon he'd felt urged to visit the chapel. Apparently, Dr. Renn was acting on her own urging to make a chapel call, and that's when she spotted Dove opening the door to the chapel. She called out to him and they walked inside together.

Willis knows what happened too—all that was said and shared, like the returned note Dove found inside the granite urn on his son's grave. "I don't understand it," he says to Dr.

Renn. "Who answered this note? Am I going crazy?" Dr. Renn will stare hard at the note in her hands, the one that contains Dove's guilt-ridden apology to his dead son on one side, and the handwriting on the back—the poignant message penned with purposeful-flourish.

Dove says, "I can't show this to Sarah or Mary-Linda. I showed it to Jay and he just shook his head. So, I came here, to ask the questions on my mind. To see if it's true what the note says."

Willis has heard every word, because he's in the chapel, too, that day, holding space for Phoebe and the impending arrival of the boy.

The storm that was *Charlie* has now moved off shore, leaving exposed Air Force Colonel Christopher Condor, the highly-decorated Air Force B52 bomber of Desert Storm.

No one has paid any attention to Willis. No one has offered to upright his cart or retrieve the supplies that rolled down the hallway to a stop in front of the auditorium double doors. As Dove, Jay, and Dr. Renn redirect Colonel Condor from the exit and toward the motoring engine within the Cooper VA, Willis uprights the cart. He gathers his fallen supplies, pausing by the auditorium doors.

George Plover has recaptured his audience. He has worked hard for this moment, deserves it, and now Plover war poetry is once again flowing throughout the auditorium and seeping through the narrow crack of the double doors. Willis smiles and walks back to his cart.

In his arms, the supplies.

In his heart, a resounding Plover-poetry-train.

In his mind, the creeping derailment—*The boy is coming*.

CHAPTER 5

FAVORITE nurse Phoebe remains locked in the past and locked up in the Cooper VA psych ward.

But every day for two weeks since his first meeting with the boy, Willis returns to the psych ward to search for Phoebe in the group room and to present her with a small bouquet of flowers. Some have been snipped from cemetery graves because in the unusual heat wave lingering over the valley early in June, they aren't likely to remain fresh for long. Willis repurposes them to help another. He also uses them in the bouquet to augment the flowers from his own garden that is still flourishing with the hummingbirds outside the east dining room. But flowers are not reaching Phoebe. And neither are the drugs or Dr. Julia Renn, although Willis can respect the doctor's tireless efforts. Phoebe is stuck in the nightmares of her past and Willis must go back to rescue this prisoner of war.

Decades earlier, someone had proposed the grand idea of offering Cooper VA psych patients the outdoors without actually having to take them outdoors. Taking them outdoors involved wheeling them, except for the ambulatory patients, to the elevators, and then down sixteen floors where along the way they could be exposed to all sorts of triggers, or become the trigger themselves for veterans who weren't patients on the psych ward, yet. Not to mention you never knew when an ambulatory patient might take flight, although every runner was eventually discovered roaming the cemetery. No one could explain why Cooper VA psych patients always ran down the hill, east, toward the cemetery. One psychologist published a paper in a medical journal and referred to this as "another morbid mystery of the mentally ill." No one at the Cooper VA was awake enough back then, and too few are now, to connect the significance of cardinal direction to the running-flight-patterns of their patients.

What does it mean? What am I missing?

Not all runners in those days waited to reach the outdoors before they took flight. When the elevator ride down sixteen floors was interrupted by doctors, nurses, other patients, or visitors and volunteers who had summoned a ride down, a psych patient with two good legs and a mind shouting *ready-set-go* might do just that. Some sprinted down the even-numbered floors. Some preferred odd-numbered floors. But anyone lucky enough to evade capture and reach the outdoors ran toward the east, and wandered among the rows and rows of white headstones.

So, architects found clever, though expensive ways to knock down a few walls between adjoining rooms on the psych ward, and replace the ceiling with glass. The Cooper VA administrator lost his job over the financial allocation of this atrium, even though someone at headquarters had granted approval from the beginning. War isn't the only scenario for lunacy, you know.

During the third week of Phoebe's residency on the psych ward, Willis turns the empty, abandoned atrium into a tropical rain forest for his favorite nurse. Doing this requires him to haul up large planters one night, along with bags of rich topsoil and a water fountain too small to accommodate a drowning. The next day, he wheels a sleepy, over-medicated Phoebe from the group room to the atrium. He parks her under the beam of outside light and leaves her in the middle of a hot, humid rain forest. He waits and watches.

Today or tomorrow.

They have eternity.

But Gray Phoebe eventually senses the light and the warmth and awakens. "Hawk," in her Phoebe-ordering-tone, "get me out of this chair." But typical of Phoebe, she is already out of the chair before he can do anything more to help her. She pushes the wheelchair away. Her eyes are Christmas-morning wide but not with joy. "Hawk, why are you doing this to me?" Since her return from Southeast Asia, Phoebe has never willingly placed herself in a tropical setting. She could go the rest of her life without looking at another palm tree or feeling the suffocating pressure of humidity. She's a no-thank-you to Bali, Bermuda, Bora-Bora, Tahiti, Hawaii, even Florida. The mountain climate surrounding the Cooper VA was as far as she could get from the past.

Phoebe's holding her arms out for him, and it takes everything Willis has not to acquiesce. He would deny her nothing.

Phoebe frantically and awkwardly attempts to unbutton both sleeves of her jumpsuit. "You know they'll be here any minute, Hawk! *You'll* be here any minute. You know what that means. I've got to be *ready-got-to-be-ready-got-to-be-ready*." She's now rolling up her sleeves, exposing what she prefers to hide—the long crisscrossing roadmapping of scars that reminds her, reminds everyone, of her 313 days as a POW. But the bulk of the jumpsuit material creates an aggravating challenge. The gray jumpsuit would be too large for Willis, let alone Phoebe, and she is wrestling with all that fabric. "I can hear the choppers, Hawk," she says, the plea in her eyes matching her tone. "The fucking choppers... they're always coming, Hawk. The fucking choppers never stop coming. Incoming, incoming, incoming...." When her sleeves are finally rolled above her elbows to suit her, she says, "Hawk, don't-make-me-don't-make-me."

She has finally pierced the heaviest gray veil, forcing them both on a journey through a long spindly astral projection that lands them just inside the main door of the 71st Evacuation Hospital in Pleiku, South Vietnam. The door has been thrust open to welcome the incoming wounded. Fear hangs heavy in the air around them, already thick with the acrid, metallic mixture of explosions and blood and dust kicked up by the wave of incoming choppers landing this second behind the hospital and the steady *thump-woosh* of the mortars and the sporadic releases of rocket fire from gunship pilots at sniper targets in palm trees. All of Pleiku appears to be on fire.

Running from the dense jungle that surrounds the evac hospital toward them is a swarm of screaming villagers, some carrying children. And several soldiers have just burst through the back doors with children in their arms and napalm on their hands and clothes.

One of the soldiers being carried on a stretcher is Willis. He is unconscious from the loss of blood. Triage will favor others with more of a fighting chance. The decision is not Phoebe's to make, but if left to her, she would make the same decision. This beautiful dark boy with the nearly severed arm—forget that hand, for it is already dead—will likely be gone before she returns from the first surgeries. A month ago, Guilt would have tugged at her heart. Not now. *Too-many-too-many-too-many.* She applies a correct tourniquet to the wrist, treats for shock by covering him with blankets, and starts an IV with a morphine dose that would have gotten her permanently kicked out of nursing. *Least I can do for him.*

A doctor covered in blood leans over to have a look at the boy on the stretcher. "Best not to think of them as bodies anymore," he says, and disappears behind doors that lead to surgery.

Phoebe, leaning over Willis, responds to no one she thinks is listening, "What are we then—a factory for the reassembly of broken toy soldiers?"

But a few hours later, the beautiful dark boy surprises Phoebe and the doctor when he is alive and stable enough for surgery. "All of them brainwashed," the doctor mutters while inspecting the tourniquet. "Trained not to quit, they can't even die in peace." He and Phoebe agree the soldier has lost too much blood and isn't likely to survive surgery, but since they're caught up anyway, they wheel him through the doors. Amputations are one of the easiest medical procedures. That's why during the Civil War, doctors just hacked away at whatever came loose on a man. Whack and hack. Hack and whack. After six months in Pleiku, Lieutenant Phoebe Kennedy has faced the worst of humanity, so the amputation of this boy's forearm and hand holds mindless consideration.

More than half of the procedures here at Pleiku involve amputations, and most involving more than one limb. Booby traps. Land mines. Grenade explosions. *How* matters little at this point.

What Phoebe doesn't yet know as this boy's arm is being amputated is how she will be forever mindfully linked to this boy. How she will wake years later in the night, and often, to his scream, "What right did you have to take what wasn't yours?" Only he's talking about much more than an arm and hand, isn't he?

What right, indeed?

But when the choppers finally leave them undefended at the 71st, and the Viet Cong emerge from the jungle, Phoebe and Willis will both look toward that pile of discarded arms and legs of soldiers in the trash container and wish for the almighty power to reassemble a platoon. The soldier—the one paralyzed and strapped in the Stryker frame and warning them of the attack—hadn't he reason to be terrified?

In the atrium, Phoebe screams and sinks to the floor. The gray jumpsuit puffs out so far from her body one could imagine a mushroom has just taken root and bloomed inside this dank rain forest. For a few moments, Willis allows her sobs. When he goes to her, sits beside her, and holds her, she finally whispers, "How do we get out of here, Hawk? Let's get out of this jungle."

Follow the Light.

She looks skyward and holds tight to him. After a few moments, he can sense the spark of Light that's finally taken hold this time, and that's growing within her. One day, he knows, she will accept that she is so much more than this one illusory life, that she is whole and innocent—and that all is forgiven and released.

We accept what we need only when we're ready to accept it.
Accept your gifts.

Two orderlies have flung open the doors to the atrium. Apparently surprised, yet relieved, to find their missing patient here, they mutter expletives between them as they advance on the gray nest of fabric and flesh and bone on the floor under the Light. "Let's get out of here, Hawk," Phoebe whispers, and squeezes his hand. "Let's go home."

CHAPTER 6

The boy is coming.

I T'S another Thursday, two weeks since the boy's first visit with his father, and this time it's shortly after three in the afternoon. This Thursday has been rainy, and the children and their parents who show up in the east dining room for a hummingbird feeding bear their disappointment. To escape the earlier downpour, the hummingbirds sought refuge among the leafy limbs of the trees down the hill toward the cemetery.

But a few minutes after the magic hour of three, the rain slacks off to a drizzle. Willis seizes the opportunity to refill the hummingbird feeders with sugar water. Behind him, the hopeful faces of two toddlers are pressed flat against the glass that he cleaned the night before, and then again this morning when the Light revealed what he'd missed.

Willis knows the boy is coming today. He's just not sure about the exact how, when, or where because the boy is returning with his parents for another counseling session with Dr. Renn. By now, the boy must itch with the desire to slip away from his parents for a chance to see the hawk. But the boy will also fear the wrath of *Charlie*.

Who wouldn't?

The drizzle ends.

A moment later, the sun breaks free. Sky-patchwork of blues is winning over grays. Willis's Monet garden shimmers under the new light and refreshed birdsong. He pours a cup of sugar water into the lid of an old Mason jar and sits on the stone bench. He waits for the hummingbirds. He glances toward the east dining room, where now the children's eyes are wide with anticipation. Others have gathered too, sensing the moment has come. All is not lost this afternoon. Relieved parents smile at other relieved parents. Everyone is waiting. Where are the hummingbirds? Eager to regurgitate the first sign of Hope, parent-eyes roam the sky and the garden, their crisscross searches mimicking the erratic flight patterns of the hummingbirds.

The boy is coming.

But so are the hummingbirds, Willis thinks, when the tiny scout arrives. The scout pauses for a sip at Willis's cup before relaying an all-clear to the others.

And here they come—an undulating cloud of color emerging from the trees and sweeping up the hill from the cemetery toward Willis's garden and toward the cheerful onlookers behind the glass of the east dining room. When the tiny birds descend upon Willis, who sits stonily in the center of a garden created out of love for Phoebe, the children behind him shriek with joy and slap the glass.

Any other day, joy would be filling up Willis too. But something has just happened.

Is it Phoebe? His hand begins to shake. A dark, oppressive heaviness is descending around him and the entire garden. The weight of the love-cup to the hummingbirds becomes too great to bear, and his hand falls to his side and hard against the seat of the stone bench, forcing the spill of the sugar water. The Mason jar lid falls to the ground and lands upside down.

And then the boy appears.

Joy turns to shrieks of fear.

Parents grab their children and usher them away from the windows.

The boy's face carries a wry smile as he approaches Willis in the garden with a snake slung like a thick black lifeline around the boy's neck and long enough to reach the baggy cargo pockets of his trousers. Dangling from the boy's left hand is the diamond-shaped head of the snake.

The boy's jarring arrival compels the flight of the hummingbirds, and they're whizzing off in so many directions that one cannot possibly guess their refuge. Willis raises his right hand to halt the boy's approach, but the boy pays no heed to Willis. The boy bears the pride of a conquering warrior.

When he's close enough, he tosses the head of the snake at Willis's feet. "The only good snake is a dead one," the boy says with pseudo confidence. He lifts the snake's body from around his neck and drops the snake's body behind the head. He lays out the body as if attempting to reassemble the poor creature. He steps back and takes a long look at his creative deconstruction. "Eight feet, I'm guessing," he says. After wiping a puddle from the stone bench, he slumps beside Willis. "You think the hawk will take him?"

Willis must measure every word. "That why you killed him—for the hawk?"

"Nah," the boy says. "I just hate snakes. Get it from my dad, I guess. He's a *grab-the-hoe-and-chop-chop-guy*, you know?" The boy laughs.

"Where you find this snake?"

"Riding around with the security guard. We saw it moving through the grass toward the bushes on the other side of the hospital." Willis knows which bushes. He planted those in the spring too. He also knows a wren has built her nest in one of them. He posted a small note on a wooden stick in front of the bush to alert the other groundskeepers of the nest to prevent a careless, fatal weed-whacking. The snake was crossing the path of the boy on its way to the eggs in the wren's nest.

Snake traveling from East toward North.

Willis sees the unfolding now. The boy doesn't have to say another word, but he will of course. In fact, the boy can't stop talking. The boy is several cups-of-words-runneth-over with Pride that he's masking as Atonement. Willis listens to the boy's description of how the security guard halted the golf cart and reached for the short wooden club he keeps behind the bench seat of the cart. "So, I say, 'Are you going to kill it?'" The guard says no and carefully walks toward the snake. The guard plans to redirect it toward the woods and away from the hospital and the bird's nest in the bushes. That's when the guard points out the small note left behind by Willis for the others. "And I say, 'Won't he just come back?'" The guard doesn't answer because he is focused on maintaining a safe distance between the snake and the end of his club, which is only three feet. The guard has the snake's attention, too, after a couple of taps with the club, and the snake coils quickly in defense. When the guard attempts to slide the snake across the green lawn back toward the woods, the curious and slightly agitated creature attempts to climb up the wooden club to reach the guard's hand. In his fearful haste to move backward, the guard stumbles and drops the club. "I keep telling him, 'Just kill it, just kill it!'" The boy leaps from the cart. What the boy leaves out of his story—and what Willis senses as most important—is that the boy's hunger for a kill has been motivated by an earlier ugly exchange with his father during the counseling session. The boy says he sprinted toward the fallen guard and kicked the back of the snake away from the club. Like his father with a hoe, the boy grabs the club and pummels the earth—his nerves and adrenalin causing clumsy misses—and the black snake is racing now toward the shelter of trees down the hill.

But Hate seeks Revenge, and a target for projection, so the boy will not give up until he exacts his pound for pound of flesh, pummel for pummel.

Snake travels from East toward North—returns North.

The natural world provides the answer when you ask the sacred questions: What does this mean? What am I missing?

When the story is over, the boy pulls a wrapped snack bar from a side pocket of his cargo trousers. "You won't have to worry about that snake now," he says, and chomps twice at the snack bar, his eyes focused on the dead snake at their feet. They sit in silence for a few moments.

The soothing gurgle of two water fountains is drowned out by a repeated car horn from the north parking lot—

probably triggered by a key fob to locate a forgotten parking spot. Willis reaches down for the snake. He hooks the body of the snake with his left, and retrieves the head with his right hand, all the while mindful to treat and hold this creature with the level of reverence it deserves. The black snake glistens like unearthed tourmaline, freshly polished.

"Aren't you going to thank me for saving your wren's nest?" the boy says and gulps down the last bite. He's wadded up the wrapper and is glancing around for a trash container. When Willis turns his back, the boy will toss the wrapper behind a bush, and Willis will retrieve it later.

"At least the snake was ethically hunting for its food," Willis says, and walks off, carrying the snake. He's halfway down the hill with the snake when he hears the boy's footsteps and heavy breathing, catching up.

The boy remains a step or two behind Willis. "So, you wouldn't care if the snake ate up all your wren's eggs?"

Willis halts and faces the boy, who recoils from the sudden nearness of the snake's body, or Willis's obvious displeasure. "The question to ask," Willis says, and raises both parts of the snake's body out to the side of his own to embody the gravity of the Separation, "is why you think the wren deserves more protection than the snake?"

The boy appears confused. "Well, that's just stupid," he finally says. "Why does the snake need protection?"

Willis thrusts the snake's head toward the boy. The boy takes another step back. "Boy, don't you know anything about snake energy—what it means to kill one? It's *you* needs protection now."

So maybe Willis went a little too far here. You be the judge. He'll admit as much afterward, and then remind himself that some people are harder than others to wake.

Some require a nudge.

Some require a shout.

Some require a thump to the head and a boot to their—.

But Willis will think about all this later, such as whether he pushed the boy too far too fast. He's witnessed Dr. Renn's mixed results. Soon as one of her veteran-patients reaches a milestone, she pushes hard for another and another and another as if Atonement is something one automatically receives after climbing to the top of Machu Picchu. Sure, a portal to Atonement might open there, and sometimes a breakthrough even occurs along the climb. Other times—a backfire that can ripple all the way back to the Cave of Creation.

For now, Willis knows what must be done to honor the spirit of the snake. He leaves the boy standing there with his young, foul mouth slack in shock and steps inside the tree line. Over a shoulder, Willis calls back, "We've got some business to attend to—get on down here."

He can feel the boy's reluctance. He can also feel the boy's curiosity. You remember—this boy is one for Knowing? He is here to Know and to spread the Knowing someday to others.

The boy is coming.

The boy's footfalls land city-dense in the natural world of the forest. He could learn a lesson or two from the fox, but that will come later. Once the boy draws near, Willis places the snake's head on the ground so that both arms are free for lifting and draping the creature's body over a low-hanging limb.

Willis drops to his knees. The warm wet earth seeps through his trousers. He rakes at the soft ground with the steel that is his left hand until he's created a small but deep depression. "Don't know what's happened to folks these days," Willis lectures as he rakes. "Serpent spirit is powerful. Respect serpent spirit, not kill it. He who kills a snake will soon see others. And he who kills another will soon be surrounded by so many snakes that they will drive a man crazy with their penetrating eyes and darting tongues, and the crazy man will never find his way out of the forest." Willis looks up at the boy who has been standing in dumbstruck silence. "Not all snakes appear in the physical, you know," he says to the boy. "Who you know got snakes in his head?" The boy doesn't answer. Willis finishes and says, "You know what to do from here."

Now the boy's eyes widen. They dart from Willis to the ground to the snake's head to its lifeless body draped over the limb and back to Willis.

But Willis stands and allows the boy the space he needs. From a nearby tree, the hawk has returned, and its shrill cries are piercing the silence between the boy and Willis.

For a moment, the boy only stares at the head of the snake. Willis will not tell him what must be done, for the boy already knows. Remembering sometimes requires a long stretch back through darkness, so Willis watches and waits. Just like with Phoebe.

Today or tomorrow.

Next week or next year.

Time is irrelevant.

Past, present, future—all happening in the Now.

Eventually, the boy's Knowing will spiral all the way back to the Light, located at the intersection of Memory and Imagination. Everyone returns to the Light in their own time. The Light is home. The Light is the birthplace of Creativity—surrounded by the on-hold, blank canvas of Nothingness.

No more than a few dozen seconds have passed, but centuries to this boy who stands in the cool-rain-drip-June-forest, with his skin crawling of goosebumps and his head itching for an immediate scrub with his left hand.

Awareness is catching up to the boy. And when it does....

The boy kneels to the earth.

But the boy still appears reluctant to lay hands on the snake. Instead, both hands vigorously scratch the itch on the crown of his head—an itch he'll never be able to reach—and he releases a growl that finally quiets the shrill cries of the hawk.

Now he is ready.

The boy reaches over and scoops both hands under the head of the snake and reverently places it in the depression created by Willis.

With both hands, the boy sweeps the earth over the depression. He creates a mound and pats the earth into place.

The boy remembers. The boy is waking.

When the boy stands, he hides his Shame-tears from Willis by lowering his head as he walks back up the hill toward the hospital. At the table where they fed the hawk, the boy slows, waits on Willis, and says, "How do you know so much about hawks and birds and snakes?"

"It's not about knowing," Willis says. "It's about *remembering* what we already know."

"Huh?" the boy says and slumps onto the bench of the table. "How can you remember something you don't already know?"

Willis chuckles. "Do you always talk in riddles?"

"Me?" the boy says, and laughs. "I looked up hawks. Do you know how many kinds there are?" Willis smiles, and the boy continues. "I can't remember enough about our hawk to know what kind. Do you know?"

"Cooper's hawk," Willis says.

The boy laughs at what he takes as a joke. "That's funny—Cooper's hawk. No, seriously. Is he a red-shoulder or a red-tail hawk?"

"Thought you said you looked up hawks. Better have another look." Just then, a lizard, oil-slick with iridescent-inky shine, climbs on the table.

Lizard climbs from South toward North.

Willis understands the powerful message of Lizard energy, and is contemplating what this means for the boy and Willis's own role in the manifestation when the boy's hand smacks hard against the table to frighten off the lizard.

Lizard runs Northwest.

Willis shakes his head.

"What?" the boy says.

"Why you do that—frighten off the lizard?" Willis, reacting to the rapid depletion of energy, leans against the edge of the picnic table.

"It's just a lizard," the boy says, and then catches himself. "Oh…."

"*Just* a lizard, *just* a snake," Willis says. "What if I was to say you *just* a boy—here you sit nearly a grown man. Where I come from, you would be a grown man by now. So, how'd that make you feel?"

The boy evades what he doesn't want to answer. "Where do you come from?"

"Same place as you," Willis says. "I come from here," and taps his head, "I come from here," and taps his heart, "and I come from here," this time opening his arms and creating several wide circles.

The boy sits silent for a moment, staring into the energy arcs of circles created by Willis. Then, "What happened to your hand? Did you lose it in the war?"

"Not the war you hoping," Willis says, knowing what pieces the boy hopes to connect back to his father. When the boy looks confused, Willis adds, "Vietnam."

"So, you killed people too," the boy says. Not quite a question, not quite a statement. He stares at his expensive shoes, and, appearing to notice the drops of snake blood, rubs one over the other as if this will erase the evidence, or the memory. "I know I'm not supposed to ask the question, Did you ever kill anyone? But did you? Will you just tell me the truth?"

The truth.

Explain truth to a boy still sleepwalking through illusions.

"Army called me a sniper," Willis finally says.

"Yeah?" The boy stares over at the north tower of the hospital, oblivious to the ruby-throated creature that is humming just above and around his head.

Hummingbird flies from South toward North, circles boy facing East, flies off North.

The boy has much yet to face.

Then, "The Air Force made my dad a bomber pilot. During Desert Storm, he killed thousands of women and children."

"And today, you killed a snake."

"That's different!" The boy clenches a fist and pounds the picnic table. "My dad killed my brother too. That's why my mother left him!" His voice is escalating and competing with the loud cries of the hawk that is circling overhead. "She blames my dad and Desert Storm—all those chemicals—for why my brother was born dead. So now I don't even have a brother and I'm stuck living with this new woman he's married to, who thinks she can do the job my mother can't do—like fix my dad. Nobody can fix my dad. Even if they could, how's that going to fix all the people he's killed, huh?"

"They're not *yours* for the fixing," Willis says. "You can only fix yourself—by loving your father."

The boy lets out a sardonic laugh. "Yeah, right." He shakes his head. "When he puts on his uniform with all those medals—I just want to rip them off. He gets medals for killing women and children. I'll leave the fixing to my step-mom—only she's not smart enough to avoid triggering—" his lips stop as they frame the beginning formation of *Charlie*. "My stepmom and the doctor..." and he completes this sentence by creating small circles around the side of his head. "They're all loco!"

Willis understands now why his impressions of the boy's mother that Sunday afternoon in Dr. Renn's office appeared less clear and strong than the impressions of the father. But he also understands that this boy has chosen this woman from before he was even born to mother him through what the boy's life-giving mother could not.

A teacher may choose the form but never the content or the student to whom the teacher will teach. These will be chosen for the teacher.

The boy glances up at the hawk. "Do you have a biscuit for him?"

"Already had his biscuit today, and if that hawk tells you otherwise, he's lying."

The boy laughs, and when he turns serious, says, "Will he eat that snake, you think?"

Willis sees the opening and knows he must seize it—another wake-up *push*. "Would that make you feel better about killing the snake?"

The boy leaps to his feet and clenches his jaw and fists. "It was just a snake, for crying out loud. You should be thanking me." This boy cut from the same Rage-cloth as his father storms up the hill in a thick billowing cloud of anger-energy that, for the first time in his life, is allowed a release without interruption. Interruption of anger plus deflection equals self-reabsorption of that anger-energy. So today, at least for today, the boy's anger storehouse will have been depleted somewhat by the time he reaches the hospital to re-form with Hurricane *Charlie*.

But the boy will return.

CHAPTER 7

O N the third Sunday in June, when Cooper VA's poet laureate is a no-show at the chapel, someone calls his home. When there's no answer, Dove and Jay pay a visit to check on their friend.

Cooper VA's poet laureate is dead.

Who is left to mourn the loss? Better yet, who is present to celebrate the life of the Battle of the Bulge warrior-poet who outlived countless friends, comrades-in-arms, parents, three siblings, a wife, a son, and a grandson? But when Cooper VA administrators remain uncooperative by workday's end on Monday, Dove Jennings and Harold Jay alert the local media to the loss of Cooper's last WWII veteran. They pitch George Plover as the personification of self-reinvention.

The newspaper and television stations recognize a great story opportunity during this particularly slow news cycle and call Cooper VA administrators to inquire how they plan to memorialize such an auspicious life.

Dumbfounded administrators call two emergency meeting sessions on Tuesday that involve a little head-and-fist-banging until someone finally calls the time and date.

Someone calls finance for line-budget advice and approval.

Someone calls the director of the funeral home that's mentioned in the obituary someone during the meeting reads aloud.

Someone calls maintenance with the urgent work order request for a white tent and a hundred white folding chairs.

Someone calls the local printer to plead for a rush job.

Someone calls a florist.

Someone calls the office manager of the cemetery.

Someone calls the chaplain who agrees to call his music programmer.

By workday's end on Tuesday, someone finally calls Dove and Jay to ask for help with the eulogy and the arrangements for a burial with full military honors.

Thursday morning at 5:55, Willis is standing in the east dining room, preparing to face the sunrise and his window-cleaning mishaps from the night before when a convoy of maintenance vehicles drives by the cafeteria wall of windows and parks in the center stretch of lawn between the hospital and the cemetery. Doors fling wide. Workers dressed in matching onesies leap to the ground and unload the vehicles. Vehicles drive quickly down the hill to the road and out of sight, leaving behind a small army of workers who, under the rosy tint of emerging light, are unraveling and erecting an enormous white tent. Willis admires the group effort. He can hear little from behind the glass, so this mass of Oneness appears to move effortlessly like a school of fish that relays mysterious insider clues to one another no outsider could ever detect.

When the sun breaks over the cemetery entrance, Willis accepts his second-chance gift of correction, and by the time he finishes, the tent is up. Depending on your perspective, the tent could appear as circus-inappropriate. Or, from the top of this slope looking down as Willis is, the tent resembles the sail of a tall ship from another era—an era even before George Plover's. So, let's pretend that George is getting a poetic sailing-send-off. Why he joined the Army and not the Navy is a mystery no one ever thought to solve. Everyone knows he returned to his family home on the outer banks and to his father's fishing business after the war. Everyone knows George grew up on a boat and learned to sail up and down the intracoastal before he was tall enough to reach the pedals of a bicycle. But no one bothered to ask George why he moved to the mountains after his wife and son and grandson left him behind.

And now no one will ever know.

Willis knows why, and glances toward the west dining room wall of windows at the mourning-lavender mountain peaks that rise like the pyramids of Egypt above their buried crystalline treasures.

The boy is coming.

Willis stashes the two biscuits he's just bought from Teana Martin in a compartment of his janitorial cart, and leaves the cart outside her cafeteria office door. His plan this morning has been to feed the hawk before the start of the memorial service, but when Teana sees him coming down the line toward her cash register with the biscuits, she releases a conspiratorial smile and produces a large envelope of prom photos.

So, no surprise that when Willis steps outside for the stroll down to the tent he discovers the hawk is circling overhead. Its cries are an out-of-tune rival for the blaring hymnal playlist selected by the chaplain that's already competing with the whirring of three industrial-sized fans brought in at the last minute because of the increasing humidity. A storm is on the way, but not until later in the day.

Willis pauses in his garden. He settles on the stone bench and closes his eyes. After a deep breath to surrender, he mindfully explains the situation to the hawk. A few still moments pass during which Willis is challenged to ignore the occasional vibrational flybys of curious hummingbirds. When he opens his eyes and glances upward all he sees is a slow-turning kaleidoscope of blue and white.

But down the hill, a steady stream of mourning is now winding toward the Cooper VA from the entrance and using every parking lot as a spillway, filling first the rows and rows and rows of handicapped spaces. In the parking lot, white-shirted security guards in golf carts offer veterans and their families a ride to the circus-tent. Some are reaching the tent by wheelchair, some by walker, some by cane, some by help of a friend's arm and a heap of patience.

At ten, everyone is in place under the tent, including two news crews from the local television stations that have set up their cameras on tripods halfway up the center aisle. Willis stands in the back. Down the hill near the cemetery entrance awaits the horse-drawn caisson with George inside a flag-draped casket and the funeral detail of young soldiers. Those with rifles have been sent on ahead, along with a young bugler.

The Navy chaplain speaks first. After the usual welcomes that acknowledge the presence of Cooper's mayor and city council members, he begins the eulogy by comparing George, small in stature but large in heart and faith, to Job. How, like Job, George's faith remained unwavering despite a string of losses that would have likely crippled the Goliaths among men. Though George Plover joined the Army at seventeen, the chaplain tells them, he never forgot his spiritual roots or his roots as a natural-born sailor of life. "George Plover, I'm sure we can agree, was a man whose compass pointed toward true north at all times." For emphasis, the chaplain points upward with an index finger.

After a lengthy prayer about the home to which George has gone and how they are to imagine the sweet and joyous family reunion, they are invited to stand and sing "Morning Has Broken" because George's wife, they are told, used to sing it every morning while preparing breakfast.

So, they sing—

> *Morning has broken, like the first morning*
> *Blackbird has spoken, like the first bird*
> *Praise for the singing, Praise for the morning,*
> *Praise for them springing fresh from the word.*

Next is Harold Jay—*Jay* to everyone who knows him. When Jay reaches the podium, he talks about George's discovery of poetry. Jay says he will be reading two of George's poems. "But before I start, I need to tell you I didn't know anything about poetry, and so I say to George one day after he's shared one of his first short poems, 'What about the rhyme, George, isn't it supposed to rhyme?' And George, see, he explains how modern poetry—*modern* poetry—" Jay pauses to allow for the eruption of laughter. "Ole George says, 'Modern poetry doesn't rhyme or sound like a nursery rhyme.' So, I'm telling *you* so the rest of you old geezers like me won't think George was a bad poet because this sure doesn't rhyme." Laughter again rolls throughout the tent.

Next is Dove Jennings, who, because of his bad hip, needs an assist up the steps from his old friend Jay. Dove begins by extending the chaplain's metaphor of George's moral compass. "George knew how to gracefully sail through the winds of change and how to use every wave for momentum. George was a man always moving forward, no matter what. When he saw you, he greeted you with, 'What's good?'" Dove says he imagines this is because George had seen enough of what's bad during the war and afterward. "He was more interested in what's good, and this was a lesson George taught me—look for the good in everything. But—" Dove's voice breaks. He reaches inside his suit coat and produces a strip of paper. He holds it up and gives it a shake for attention. "George taught me other lessons too. I've only shared this with a few people—" He pauses a moment to tamp down the reverberations of emotion that are getting the best of him. He begins again, "One day I was visiting my son's grave— *our* son's grave," he corrects and nods toward Sarah who is sitting in the second row beside Jay's wife, Becky. "Maybe like some of you, one day I left a note behind for my son. I don't know why. I just felt like it, you know? So, I stuffed the note inside the urn and left. One day I go back, and this time I decide to take the note out because I think maybe seeing my note there will upset my wife when she goes there to replace the flowers, you know? And that's when I discover that someone's answered my note to my son." Dove raises the slip of paper and waves it in the air.

Heads are turning. The volume on whispers is quickly increasing. Willis feels his heart quicken and his mind race with rare unease. What else is Dove Jennings about to reveal? With a glance around the tent, Willis's eyes land on the boy who is sitting a few rows to the right. The boy is dressed in a navy blazer and white shirt and sits beside his father who also wears a navy blazer and white shirt. The boy has spotted Willis at the same time, or perhaps the boy summoned Willis's attention, but the boy smiles. Willis forces a smile against the pressures of his accelerating heart and mind about what Dove Jennings could say next. The boy has nudged his father and is pointing his father's attention toward Willis. The father swivels in his chair and leans ahead of and behind the other turning heads to find Willis and gives up the search when Dove's voice booms through the microphone with renewed energy.

"*That answer* on the other side of the note to my son, folks, is the reason I'm still here today. *That answer* could only have been written by someone with a large and caring heart—and with the mind of a *poet.*" He pauses here, as if to allow his words the weight of resonance. And then, "So one day, I showed *George* the note, and I say, 'George—you did this, didn't you? You left this note for me.' Of course, everybody knows George Plover has never taken credit for any help he's ever given anyone, and he wasn't about to start that day. So, Ole George—he just smiles and walks off. Just smiles and walks off. Now I ask you—how many others here found a note like this from inside the cemetery urn belonging to a loved one buried down the hill? I sure hope you kept it because it was written by our dear friend and poet George Plover."

What? That's not what happened!

Here's what happened. A week earlier, Willis was heading outside to feed the hummingbirds and passed Dove and George in the east dining room. Dove stops George and thrusts a note toward the old soldier. Willis hears Dove question George about the note, and slows his walk toward the garden so that he can listen in on the exchange, and he detects a quick flash of confusion. George instinctively tilts his left ear with the hearing aid toward Dove as if to catch what words might still be lingering in the small space between them. And when they weren't lingering there, George, not being the type to trouble people to repeat themselves on his account, smiles and hurries off, leaving Dove Jennings to believe he's heard what he wants to hear, or needs to hear, even though he hasn't actually heard a word.

Interpretation is not fact.

But from the center of the tent, an arm is slowly extending and reaching upward as a witness to George Plover's cemetery-sentiments.

Another arm goes up from the right side of the tent.

Now from the left.

Arms are reaching upward from the back rows.

Men's arms.

Ladies' arms.

Another and another.

For the first time in a long time, Willis isn't crystal clear on what he's supposed to do, or what he's supposed to think for that matter. Surely he'll have to allow byline credit now to be extended to George Plover, and he'll have to accept that his own role in returning comfort to those who leave notes at graves will have to end if he's to help perpetuate the legend of George Plover. But how does Willis really feel about this?

Sad.

He'll miss reading the notes and extending small measures of comfort. In a way—he feels as if he's just entered a new unexplored ring of the Void. He needs refuge—a quiet spot for allowing the answers that can only flow to him in the stillness. But he and the boy have locked eyes again and this time the boy is pointing upward. He grins as if he's letting Willis in on another secret. Willis looks to the top of the tent and sees that a yellow butterfly is circling them. The boy is still grinning when the father leans over and whispers something that causes the evaporation of Joy. Dark turns back to face the front of the tent.

Dove's voice booms over them, "Thank you for sharing your witness of the miracle that was our friend George Plover." Released, the arms quickly drop. "So today we mourn the loss of our friend, George, but we celebrate the gifts he shared with us, and we carry the legacy of those gifts within each of us."

After the final prayer, Willis has to jump aside as they spring from their seats and seek the flow of least resistance. The tent is leaking Hope.

Where there is hope, there is life.

Mourners stream down the banks of the wide, green lawn toward the stone-columned cemetery entrance where George Plover on his horse-drawn carriage awaits the ride to the plot he chose more than a decade ago after his grandson committed suicide in Germany. You see, George felt his grandson should be rested beside his grandmother, so George offered his own plot to his grandson's widow, and the German-widow readily accepted. So, George had to reserve another plot—the one he's on his way to today.

You're supposed to follow respectfully behind the horse-drawn caisson with the flag-draped casket, but many of these mourners are acting as if they've never attended a military funeral. They feign a respectful pace toward dead-George, but soon as they clear the carriage, they're off. It's a comical footrace. Willis stands at the top of the hill and watches the spectacle. In another lifetime, perhaps he would have felt Guilt or Remorse for his role in all this, but not today. He's still spiraling around that new ring of Void, trying to grab hold of the idea that his note-writing days are truly over. In this lifetime, he has learned to accept and to allow many things, but this one—he can't help but shake his head.

Below him, it's an Easter egg roll for adults without Easter or the eggs. They're down there pulling dead flowers or plastic ones from the granite urns and reaching inside. "Got one!" shouts someone from behind a copse of trees, and Willis knows who it is because he knows the placement of every grave and every note. Most are coming up empty handed, of course, because most have never written a note. But you have to admire their hope. People, especially cynics, are so thirsty for miracles. Despite what they say, they secretly wish to be proven wrong. But the cynical ones are those who haven't yet overcome feeling betrayed by their parents and belittled by childhood friends who learned first the truth about Santa, the Tooth Fairy, and the Easter Bunny. *Prove it*, the cynical ones now say to everything. *Can you prove it?* Never mind that most of what was proven fifty years, or hundreds of years, ago has already been disproved.

Nothing moves faster than the speed of light, they'll say, as a way to affirm the impossibility of visits to Earth from other worlds. Try explaining quantum physics—how time is not actually linear, how we can actually rewrite the history of our future—and their heads will spin until their eyes nearly pop out of their heads. Warn them about impending entropy or talk to them about the only solid solution for humanity, which is to elevate the collective consciousness—how we are all connected to one another through thought—and get the same reaction. But a time is coming. And even the cynical ones know this, for no one can *un*-know what they already know.

They can only refuse to Remember.

"Hey, wait up."

The Voice belongs to the boy. He is carrying the navy blazer in his left hand as he jogs down the road of the cemetery toward Willis. "Have you fed the hawk today?"

"You got time to help me feed the hawk?" Willis starts walking again. He's a half-step ahead, and the boy is trying to match the cadence. Willis's long stride makes the march a difficult one, so the boy has to hop-skip every third step to keep up.

"My dad's going to be tied up with some group thing for a couple of hours. He gave me money for lunch in the cafeteria." The boy fishes in his pocket and withdraws a crumpled twenty-dollar bill. "So, can I help you feed the hawk? I've got a lot of questions, if you don't mind me asking. I looked up hawks again—you know—like you said, and there really is a Cooper's hawk. That's crazy, you know? A Cooper's hawk here at Cooper."

"What else you learn about Cooper's hawk?" Willis says, and smiles. They're close enough to Teana's cafeteria to smell her something-Italian lunch special.

"I can't remember everything, but the coolest thing is Cooper's hawks protect hummingbirds. Did you know that?"

The boy races ahead of Willis through the garden, oblivious to the whizzing hummingbird and butterfly energy around him. When he reaches the exterior door of the east dining room, he holds it open for Willis. "No one knows why," the boy says, following Willis inside, "about Cooper's hawks protecting hummingbirds. Hawks usually eat other birds. Why do you think Cooper's hawks protect hummingbirds?"

Willis pauses at the stack of cafeteria trays. Lingering in the air with the boy's curiosity is the aroma of Teana Martin's eggplant parmesan and her peal of laughter emanating from the direction of the cash register, but the boy has spotted the pizza station and off he goes. While the boy winds his way with a tray through the cafeteria line, Willis retrieves the biscuits from his janitorial cart. He would have preferred a few moments in stillness to reflect on George's memorial service and Dove's Revelation-that-wasn't. He would have preferred to visit Phoebe. He would have preferred time alone with the hawk.

But this is what happens when you fail to check in on a regular basis: you fall out of touch with Awareness.

Outside at the picnic table the boy folds the giant slice of cheese pizza and takes a bite. As a spurt of grease tinged orange by tomato sauce travels down his chin toward his white shirt, the boy drops the pizza slice on the plate, collects the grease in his hand and, realizing he's forgotten napkins, is about to wipe his hand across his lap when a white handkerchief dangles in front of his face. "Thanks," he says with a full mouth of pizza and wipes off the grease. The boy glances from his sky-searches for the hawk to the business of biscuit shredding that's happening on the table beside his slice of pizza. "Was it hard at first?" the boy asks and stares at the black whirl of steel as the hook that is Willis's left hand rips apart the bread.

"Nothing's hard when you learn to get out of your own way," Willis says and begins the shredding process of biscuit two.

"What does that mean—getting out of your own way?" The boy rips another hunk from the pizza and this time isn't fast enough to catch the orange blob of grease and sauce that reaches his white shirt. "Aw, man!" He dabs at the grease stain with Willis's handkerchief and seeing the spread of orange stain, gives up.

"Best to show that stain to your stepmother soon as you get home," Willis says, "so you can save that shirt."

The boy shrugs.

"What you got against that woman, anyway?"

The boy answers with another shrug.

"You're full up with talk when you get to choose the subject." Willis has finished shredding the second biscuit. He sweeps all the crumbs together, forming a small white mountain.

When Willis moves to the opposite end of the table, the boy slides down too. He's about to take the final bite of his lunch when the hawk announces his arrival with a shrill call. The boy drops the pizza. They look up and find the hawk circling overhead.

"Do you think he'll come?" the boy says around the final mouthful.

"Are you asking him to come?"

"What do you mean—talk to him?" And when Willis nods, the boy laughs and says, "It's not like he's a dog, like I can go, 'Come here, Hawk,' and 'Good boy!'"

"Why not?"

The boy grins and makes the circle gesture for *crazy.* "You want me to talk to the hawk...*you* talk to the hawk."

"I talk to the hawk every day," Willis says. "Bet he'd like to hear from somebody new."

The boy lets out a howling laugh. When he looks upward for the hawk and sees nothing but clouds, he turns serious. "Where did he go?" He unfolds himself from the picnic table bench and steps from the shadow of shade under the junipers and long-leaf pines. Shielding his eyes against the sun with both hands, the boy appears to be holding a pair of binoculars, and, turning slowly in a full circle to scan the skies as if the watcher of an incoming air raid, he finally comes full circle and drops his arms by his side. "Where did he go?"

"Don't you know?"

"Know what?" The boy returns to the table under the shade and releases Frustration by retrieving his blazer that has fallen to the grass under the bench and throwing it in a heap on the table. But Willis says nothing. Willis allows the moment of silence to seep inside the boy's consciousness and marry itself with Regret. Since Regret resides so close to the surface of this boy's skin, as it does most everyone's, it needs only a whisper of an invitation. Willis's Patience will be rewarded when this moment of silence is finally interrupted by the boy's sober, "Should we try to call him? Will he come if we call him?"

"Nothing hurt by trying."

The boy cups his hands around his mouth to form a megaphone for shouting when Willis grabs the boy's shirt sleeve to stop him. "Not that way," Willis says. "Use your head." The boy's face registers with confusion, so Willis adds, "With your mind…with your thoughts."

"That doesn't make sense," the boy says. "How will he hear me?"

"I don't got all day to spend feeding this hawk. Either you going to call him back here or we sweep off the pile of crumbs for the other birds. And you get back to your father." Willis feigns a move toward the opposite end of the table to sweep off the crumbs.

"Wait—I mean, how do you do it?"

So picture this—

Willis and the boy are sitting beside one another at the round picnic table under the dark shade of the tall evergreens with their backs to the Cooper VA. Their eyes are closed. Willis provides measured instruction on the art of breathing. They take two command breaths, which are two deep breaths held several seconds while tensing every muscle in their bodies, until Willis says *Release*. After the two command breaths, they'll take a breath to surrender. "The breath to surrender," Willis says, "leads to a quiet void in the mind, a void all the way back to Nothingness."

The boy interrupts, of course. "How can he hear us if our minds are in nothingness?" And Willis returns the explanation that the only way to reach the hawk is to join him in the Nothingness. "But what do I say when I get there—in the Nothingness?"

"Nothing," Willis says. "Speak through your heart. When you reach the Nothingness, place your right hand over your heart and feel—feel the hawk with your heart." The boy practices by placing his hand over his heart, shrugs, and closes his eyes again.

And then the two of them start over with two deep command breaths that, with Willis's guidance, will lead them to the longer breath they hold several seconds before releasing in total surrender. Picture the two of them covering their hearts with their right hands. Picture them searching for the way to Nothingness—a journey much easier for the boy at his age than would be for most adults their first time, especially for the boy's father.

Now picture Willis and the boy entering the Nothingness together. Picture them feeling with heart navigation throughout the Nothingness for the hawk, so deep in their Nothingness search that they are unaware that clouds surrounding the Cooper VA have moved across the path of the sun. The air has cooled and the breeze, much stronger than earlier, has carried off the boy's pizza-stained paper plate, sending it like a whirling dervish into the forest where Willis will discover it hours later a few feet west of the snake's burial site.

And *now…now* picture this—the boy whispers, "He's coming." And then, like an underwater diver who has been furiously kicking his way to the surface, the boy returns all the way up from the Nothingness, and his eyes grow wide and bright. He shrieks, "He's coming!" When he leaps from the table, he bumps hard into Willis. The boy stands in the opening beyond the trees and searches the skies that have grown dark and are producing long rolls of rumbling thunder.

Willis knows their time here is down to minutes, but *what* minutes they will be for this boy, for them both. Joy fills Willis as he watches the boy spin clockwise, lingering a second here and there at each cardinal point of direction to search for the hawk. "I can *hear* him. Can you hear him?"

Willis can, of course, hear the hawk, but this moment belongs to the boy.

"There!" the boy shouts, and points south. "There!"

Hawk flies from South toward East.

"We did it! He heard us!" The boy becomes an air traffic controller as his arms wave the hawk in for a landing, and when it's clear the hawk is on the correct line of approach, the boy's feet hardly touch the ground in his clockwise sprint back to the table. Without any coaching from Willis this time, the boy stands with quiet reverence at a table set for a hawk, with whom this boy has joined in the majesty of Nothingness and called forth with his heart.

And don't you know Willis wishes his only handkerchief weren't lying there on the picnic table in a wadded orange bundle of pizza grease?

CHAPTER 8

THURSDAY afternoons thereafter become standing appointments between Willis and the boy. Each Thursday afternoon, the boy somehow manages to escape either the beginning or the ending of whatever Dr. Renn is offering in the way of family counseling, and Willis assumes that all is happening according to The Plan. The boy somehow always knows where to find Willis, though Willis helps a great deal most Thursdays by finding excuses for hanging around the garden outside the east dining room or even inside the dining room, waiting. And since the boy usually shows up around one, Willis has explained to the hawk the reasoning behind adjusting the biscuit-feeding schedule, and the hawk appears compliant.

On Thursdays when group sessions for the boy's father and stepmother extend well past three, Willis allows the boy to help with the hummingbird feeding. The boy knows now which refrigerator in Teana Martin's kitchen holds the special sugar-water concoction. He knows the precise water to sugar percentages when new batches must be prepared, how to boil and cool, and which plastic tubs Teana Martin has set aside and labeled with a black marker, **HUMMINGBIRDS**.

Even though Teana Martin says every time the boy appears in her kitchen, "Now you know you're not allowed back here—no minors are allowed in my kitchen," she always punctuates this statement with a wink. Teana Martin laughs even more easily these days. Her daughter has graduated from high school and is so distracted with a new boyfriend and preparations for college that Teana has just enough freedom for the first time in eighteen years to allow *herself* a boyfriend. Willis likes the young man who manages a tire store in Cooper and occasionally visits Teana during his lunch breaks and has promised to outfit Teana's car with four discounted tires before she drives her daughter over the mountains to college.

Every Thursday, the boy arrives with a head full of questions, and this Willis accepts and allows too, because the boy is here for the purpose and path of Knowledge—though the boy hasn't fully remembered this yet. On this particular Thursday, Willis is sitting at the picnic table after helping the boy call for the hawk and listening to the boy share his knowledge about geology from a book he's been reading over the summer. The boy loves reading. While too many kids his age are head-buried in some sort of electronic gadget that dulls one's vibrational frequency, this boy is head-buried in knowledge-gathering.

But today, the boy's noticeably edgier than usual. He's been fidgeting and talking rapidly in that way people do when they fear being interrupted, and since feeding the hawk, the boy has been shooting glances toward the exit door of the north tower of the Cooper VA. Willis knows the boy is watching for his father's impatient *let's-go* signal, and each Thursday, the boy leaves with greater reluctance, possibly dragging behind him the weight of Willis's own disappointment. Willis has become fond of the boy. What felt ominous months ago when he began sensing the coming of the boy has been replaced with a sense of auspicious responsibility for the path of this chosen one. But whatever help Dr. Renn is offering Colonel Condor and his wife doesn't seem to be easing the boy's anxiety, which has turned as sour-palpable as the tall glasses of Teana's lemonade sweating on the picnic table during today's lecture from the boy about what textbook explanations he's discovered—shifting of tectonic plates that eventually divided Earth into seven continents, about the formation of mountains and the role that friction plays in creation—

Now.

Willis senses his opening. He hears the Voice, and while he would so much more prefer to listen to the boy's excited ramblings about his discoveries, however archaic, Willis feels the pressing urge to seize this moment. He sighs, and then after another breath says, "Like friction with your father?"

If Willis had thrown his glass of lemonade in the boy's face the boy couldn't have appeared more stunned, and then more agitated. The once excited energy transforms to Dark. "What are you talking about?"

"That part you said—about friction playing a role in creation. What are you trying to create with the friction with your father, you think?"

The boy shoots another glance toward the north tower. "I don't want to talk about him. I've told you that before. Why do you always bring him up?"

Willis takes a long drink of his lemonade and shakes the wetness from his right hand. "I can't remember the last time we talked about your father." Of course, Willis knows why the boy feels they talk about his father all the time—because Willis is always talking to the boy through thought in the way Willis and the boy talk to the hawk—from their heart-language inside the Nothingness. There, the boy calls for the hawk while Willis speaks to the boy about Self-forgiveness, and about Compassion and Love for his father. You see, the boy cannot fulfill his assignment here without a letting go of the older karmic-building energy that no longer serves a purpose. And this is what Willis must help the boy see—that his purpose is higher and requires a higher level of consciousness.

"I hate coming here," the boy blurts out. He grabs his glass of lemonade and walks to the edge of the woods, tossing out the contents. On the way back to the table, he says, "At least the ants will be happy today."

"Being happy is a choice," Willis says after the boy has slammed the glass back to the table—a slam Willis feels all the way to his heart. Willis wouldn't choose to upset the boy, or to upset what has been a lovely afternoon to this point. Willis would have preferred to have listened to the boy lecture on and on about his geological discoveries. Today is cooler than usual for late June, and the branches of the junipers and pines that divide the Cooper VA expanse of lawn from the cemetery are dancing with abandon. Why purposely ruin the spellbound magic of such an afternoon?

Teaching is the hardest job he's ever taken on—much harder than being an Army sniper—and Willis often wonders why he agreed, why anyone would welcome such an auspicious hardship, especially when not allowed to choose your own students.

"Happy is a choice?" the boy says and glances at the north tower before climbing atop the picnic table, something he's never done before. He stands on the table and extends both arms outward, forming a small т. "Tell that to my father, will you?" The arms fall. The boy slumps into a cross-legged heap on the table and drops his head in his hands. "I'm so tired of coming here. I'm so tired of pretending that everyone here is a hero. I'm just so tired of pretending to appreciate what they call *sacrifice* when it's just killing and killing and killing." The boy looks up with a face that's growing tear-stained. "Will it ever end, Willis? The killing?"

Oh yes, Dear One! And you are here to help end the killing!

But it's important to pause here for the recognition that this is the first time the boy has uttered Willis's name. You see, Willis's shirts don't bear the embroidered nametag or plastic name plate as everyone else's at the Cooper VA, but the boy has surely heard and remembered Teana Martin saying things such as, "*Willis*—why you bring that boy back here to my kitchen? You trying to get me fired?" or "*Willis*—you train that boy right on how to feed Cooper's hawk and those precious hummingbirds now, you hear?" Still, the boy has never uttered, Willis, until this very moment, and the sound of "Willis" from the boy's mouth resonates with the perfect toning-harmonic vibration of a musical C note within Willis's entire Spirit.

So, in response to the boy's question, Willis hears himself say, "Yes, one day you will stop the killing."

"I'm not doing the killing," the boy shouts. "They are!" He points toward the hospital, and then fires Anger toward

Willis. "And you!" The boy launches a tirade about how he's sick and tired of pretending to respect people who have killed others, or those who are willing to kill others. About how different his life would be, could be, if his father had never joined the military and come home as someone different.

How to explain?

Eli…the boy-chosen has chosen this experience. We create our own realities. It's not what happens to us but how we choose to respond.

"Why do we even have to have a military?" the boy says. "What if we all just said *no*, we're not going to have a military? Doesn't *anyone* ever think about this?"

"All the time," Willis says.

"Then why does anyone ever join the military in the first place? Why don't we all just say no? What's the government going to do? Put us all in jail? You can't jail an entire country!" The boy scratches the top of his blond head that's been sheared for the summer in a military buzz cut. He's remembering something….

That's the hardest part, you know. Remembering why you're here. The oldest of us, and we're not referring to age, aren't afraid to ask, *Why am I here?* We're the ones walking through life with the nagging complaint that we seem to have misplaced or forgotten something. An hour into a cross-country flight, we're the ones still anticipating the sudden jolt of remembrance that comes with what we forgot to pack or what we, regrettably, forgot to turn off or unplug. And when words like shampoo, razor, toothpaste, or coffee pot pop into memory, we accept that the mental search was worthwhile, even though we know the activity of the search—the steady *practice* of searching, if you will—should be leading to something much more profound. With practice like this, however, we get better at remembering the most important thing—what we swore we would remember this time around. And we all do, eventually. We wish, however, to remember before it's too late to render much usefulness with the remembering. We swear during the joyous reunion celebration that awaits us on the other side of the veil that we'll do better next time. And we're the ones who quickly beg for another try. *Put me back in, Coach!* Because who wouldn't want to return here to play this beautiful Game, even though we'll have to leave a piece of our ever-expansive loving selves on the other side?

How to recognize the oldest of old souls? We're the ones with the lowest of low Worth, like Phoebe and others here at the Cooper VA, because we remember the consequences of our mistakes from thousands and thousands of lifetimes.

But a shift has finally ushered in the revolution-evolution, so now some of the oldest souls are, like this boy, still under twenty. No longer are the elders the guaranteed wisdom-holders. The oldest souls among the elders know this already and are making the shift. The youngest souls among the elders will flail about in the old energy, but they will return here one day wiser. *This* boy, oldest of old souls, has returned with a special assignment this time—choosing wisely his parents and the circumstances that will enhance his learning and permit him an even larger footprint this time on humanity. For this task, he brings with him all his other selves—including the peacemaker, including the warrior. But Hate threatens to lead the boy astray.

Enter Willis. At least this is what Willis supposes since not even he has all the answers.

"You're allowing Hate to lead," Willis says with a tone meant to indicate a warning he hopes the boy will hear and heed. "Want to change the world? Lead with your heart—like with the hawk."

"Yeah, right. No thank you." The boy leaps from the table and marches up the hill toward the north tower, perhaps forgetting the door is locked from the outside. Just then, the boy apparently remembers the locked north tower door, or he connects with Willis's thoughts, because the boy right-flanks for the long stroll around the north tower that will lead him back to the main entrance of the Cooper VA and to the celebrated Hall of Heroes with its framed photographs paying homage to all those young warriors from Cooper who gave their all for others, including one warrior the boy knows but who the boy will not, cannot, see, on the wall because the boy's head remains downward all the way to the elevator that will deposit him outside Dr. Renn's suite of offices where *Charlie* has been ugly-arguing so loudly for a half-hour that security guards with name badges and clubs have been silently alerted and stand nearby with two bruiser-big orderlies Willis recognizes from the psych ward.

One day the boy will see himself, the warrior, on that wall, and....

All this Willis can see while the cool June breeze sweeps over and around and through him because all this has already happened, although the boy just now disappears around the corner of the north tower.

CHAPTER 9

FOR more than two months now Phoebe has been locked inside the psych ward of the Cooper VA hospital with the screamers and the feces-graffiti-artists. Since her lock-up, spring in the valley that lies at the foot of the Blue Ridge Mountains has completed its transformation to full summer. The days are longer now and the cemetery is overrun with evening walkers—mostly Cooper VA nurses during dinner shifts or breaks, or the Cooper VA dedicated volunteers who change shoes for a quick stroll over the cemetery's hills and along its intricate, web overlay of narrow footpaths before heading home to their other lives. In the moments leading toward each sunset, a grandiose pause occurs. All eyes gaze west and a hush descends over the cemetery. Perhaps this is the moment walkers first become aware of the symphony of cicadas over which the walkers have been talking or mind-chattering. Perhaps they finally acknowledge the circling overhead of the Cooper's hawk, or let loose a chuckle at the croaking bullfrog from the retention pond.

Then again, perhaps not. Even awake, most are asleep, or sleepwalking through their illusions of self-creation. But at sunset, they stand quietly surrounded by a symbolic hemisphere of Death, and witness each day's resplendent ending, unconsciously aware that what they are choosing is to face their own fears of Death. We ask you to think of Death as figurative. You might as well, for to think of Death in any other way other than as the magnificent manifestation of another beginning—your beginning—is to think with too small a mind, and you are so much more than this.

Just as Phoebe was beginning to remember, thanks to her trip to Memory with Willis in the atrium-Vietnam jungle, Dr. Renn ordered a psychotropic cocktail-double for Phoebe, believing that keeping Phoebe drugged and her presence accounted for every second of the day and night was best for everyone's favorite nurse. Actually, Dr. Renn was afraid of witnessing her own figurative death at the Cooper VA if anything other than a full recovery were to befall Cooper's favorite nurse. For months, Dr. Renn has denied Dove Jennings and Harold Jay access to Phoebe. They, however, have been relentless. They were Marines at the Chosin Reservoir, after all. How are Dr. Renn's objections to their seeing Phoebe anything other than annoying and minor skirmishes? With every request to see Phoebe they wear down Dr. Renn's resolve. Willis can also hear Weariness clawing at her voice these days during her repeated justifications to administrators, veteran-patients, and families regarding her methods. Make no mistake— every doctor and administrator at the Cooper VA *wants* a cure to what causes their veteran-patients to spin off into frightening Darkness, sometimes failing to return. When spouses complain to Dr. Renn behind closed-door sessions that don't include their veteran-spouses, or during secret telephone calls to complain that all their veteran-spouses do is sleep fourteen to sixteen hours a day, Dr. Renn says, "Be thankful." Willis knows why too. Why she stayed in the chapel for nearly an hour after Dove left that day. How she walked to the altar, knelt, and unleashed Anger. How the shaking from sobs afterward reduced her to a puddle at the foot of that altar. You see, Dr. Renn was responding to the earlier discovery that one of her veteran-patients had taken himself off his medications after his wife complained one time too many times about his constant check-out. Finally checking back into their life, the veteran-patient, still unwilling to forgive himself and others—decided that life itself was too difficult—correction, *meaningless*—so he checked back out, for good this time, but not until he'd shot and killed his wife too.

The finger-pointing begins immediately, of course, because it will take weeks for the toxicology report to reveal that the veteran-patient suddenly halted all his medications in an attempt to appease his wife. And during the weeks-long waiting period, Cooper VA administrators launch their usual investigation. So adept are they all now at these investigations that when the young investigator appears in the doorframe of her office bearing a face full of apology, Dr. Renn silently hands over the current password to her computer that will provide him access to every single one of her patient files, and walks out. Willis, in the hallway outside her office that morning, sees the tears and hears her sobs all the way down the long hall, feels the gravity behind the push she lands on the exit door of the stairwell, and hears the wails of Frustration and Sadness during her descension into Unworthiness for at least two floors. Where she will go he isn't sure, but at 3:33 that afternoon, she pushes her way into the garden from the door of the east dining room and marches down the hill toward the cemetery without so much as a glance toward Willis who was, before her interruption, immersed in a mesmerizing cloud of hummingbird-bliss, to the delight of those watching on the other side of the dining room windows.

But an hour from now, Dr. Renn, Dove Jennings, and Willis will wander into the Cooper chapel—each seeking an individual answer from the same sacred questions, *What does it mean?* and *What am I missing?*

This explains why Phoebe, in fact why all the psych ward patients these days in the wake of the recent veteran-patient murder-suicide, now spend their days in dopey-land. "Better dopey than dead," Willis overhears Dr. Renn whisper to a nurse when issuing orders to increase medication levels.

Phoebe spends most of her dopey days now in a chair beside one of the barred windows in the group room, unreachable even by Willis who relentlessly calls to her from the beautiful Nothingness the way the boy called for the hawk. He visits her every day too. If it were up to him, Willis would scoop Phoebe into his arms and carry her from this place forever. But it's not up to him. So, he continues to show up every day with flowers that she looks through and never appears to see or smell. He searches her stare for a glint of recognition. He longs to hear "Hawk." Twice he manages to sneak her past the orderlies and back to the atrium-jungle, hopeful there she will return to him and their past as before, and to manifest the same homeward request. In the atrium-jungle he holds her hand, whispers in each ear that she's so much more than this—reminding her that the brain is not *her*, that the brain is not her *mind*—and he pleads with her to remember that her mind has the power to overcome anything, including the effects of medication, let alone its strength to defeat the forces of Dark that have been advancing since that one single action she took in Vietnam to save an Army sniper with a bounty on his head from agonizing, humiliating enemy torture. Anyone with half a heart would have done the same. So, Willis whispers over and over…*I'm here. It's Hawk. I'm still here, Phoebe.*

Not until the investigation finally reveals the cause of the murder-suicide of Dr. Renn's veteran-patient was the unmistakable result—or *mistakable*, in this case—of the veteran-patient halting all his medications without her approval does the heavy gray veil begin to lift from the psych ward of the Cooper VA. Willis, still visiting Phoebe every day, gleans flashes of the Light of Phoebe. Yesterday while sitting in the sunlight funnel from the barred windows, she actually turned her attention toward the colorful bouquet of flowers that seemed to appear from nothingness. Today, she opens her mouth in an oval-shaped attempt to form *Hawk*. She is returning, yes, but only to another starting point for the work against her shadow self that hides in the corners of Dark. Only a journey all the way back to the Self can coax the shadow toward the Light, and the way back can be an arduous process. They had been so close that first afternoon in the atrium-Vietnam before the orderlies burst upon them.

Even Willis sometimes feels the sting of Impatience.

Phoebe's only authorized visitors are Dove Jennings and Harold Jay, and they were only today authorized a visit after another contentious debate with Dr. Renn. Anyone in the hallway that afternoon might have deciphered Dove's and Jay's well-meaning concerns for Phoebe as threats to Dr. Renn's medical career at Cooper, or beyond. After all, for months they've been asking for, then arguing for, access to their favorite nurse who for decades here at Cooper has been every veteran's favorite nurse. Please know that Dr. Renn means well. Anyone can see this, especially Willis. She's caught between the backbreaking wall of an immoveable VA system and the potential triggering of her patients that could spiral them toward a suicidal or murderous outcome. Dr. Renn, as with the rest of her colleagues here and around the medical profession, is limited by the practice of *legal* outcome-based medicine, and although Dr. Renn is willing to try all sorts of homeopathic courses such as writing workshops, drumming, art therapy, and Tibetan singing bowls, she's also protective of her favorite nurse.

But Dove, refreshed and inspired by the impact he's had on others since his confessed revelation at George Plover's memorial service, has convinced Harold Jay to join him in the argument for seeing Phoebe. And all this Willis hears, as does everyone else who curiously wanders from their offices toward the center of the hallway at the urging escalation of Anger and Frustration.

The next day Dr. Renn apparently grants Dove and Jay special permission because Willis is outside the east dining room refilling the hummingbird feeders and sees Harold

Jay pushing Phoebe in a wheelchair down the road that connects the hospital to the stone-columned entrance of the cemetery. Dove, with that bad hip of his that he refuses to let Cooper VA surgeons correct, is limping alongside them. Occasionally he bends over to say something to Phoebe. Even from this distance, Willis can tell that Phoebe isn't responding the way Dove has hoped she would.

Soul retrieval isn't for the faint of heart, you know. Willis has twice in two months come close to retrieving Phoebe's, but once you let Dark win—even for a moment, let alone the series of small victories over your lifetime—the extraction from Dark becomes far more challenging. And that's where he is with Phoebe. Close as Willis has come to retrieving her, she's tired, you know? She's tired of justifying her human heart in conflict with the Self. Tired from decades of running and hiding from Memory. Tired of feeling separated from Self because she's been searching externally for Worth in the eyes of every veteran-patient since Vietnam, and especially in the eyes of every Vietnam veteran. And who can blame her? How hard it is to face and accept that our outward circumstances reflect our inward selves. How hard it is to accept that each of us has the power to create our own realities. Part of this is accepting that it's not what happens to us but how we choose to respond that shapes and creates our realities. So much easier to claim and believe that our brains are broken, or that we are broken, or that life itself is broken—none of which is ever fixable.

How difficult it is to accept that the spark of Divine Creation infused within each of us before we emerge from the Cave of Creation never goes out, meaning that each of us can overcome the belief we have nothing more to offer; or the belief we have been forsaken and separated forever from those on the other side of the veil; or the belief we'll never remember where we misplaced the key for Imagination that unlocks the Memory chamber, housing everything we need for accomplishing the humanity-saving work for which each of us is here. Instead, we'd rather believe we're too broken to save anything, and might as well give up the search. After all we've done to others, after all we've witnessed that's been done to others, aren't we *all* just Worthless?

Wake up, Phoebe.

It's Hawk, Phoebe. Wake up. Accept your gifts.

The others on the psych ward who paint on the walls of the group room, as well as all the forthcoming self-imprisoned by Dark still driven to create art even with their feces, are attempting to reconnect themselves with the innate—the field of celebratory, energetic Worth of the I Am. *What* is the gift?

The innate ability to heal ourselves.

It's always there, you know. Sometimes we've buried our innate healing ability under a thousand lifetimes of Guilt and Regret or we've buried it under an avalanche triggered by this life's landslide of both. But those with even the slightest Memory of the gift are the ones who use Creativity like a jackhammer of vibration, and they pulverize one boulder after another into harmless dust. Creativity, the action of Creation, allows the recalibration of every molecule, which has, after all, an epicenter of Creation. Once activated, every molecule of our being reconnects and joyously vibrates with the All that is, was, and ever will ever be.

So—let the veteran-patients create.

Let them create with paint, crayons, pencils—their own blood if need be.

Let them sculpt.

Let them sing. Play guitars. Bang piano keyboards and slap drums.

Let them whistle out-of-key tunes.

Let them hum and chant with Tibetan monks and singing bowls or to a melodic, harmonic frequency only they can hear.

Let them dance or twirl like a whirling-Rumi.

Let them string crystalline beads like words into stories… even into bad poetry like George Plover's…or into Psalms or songs of remembrances.

Let them string words into metaphors with vibrational profundity.

Let them sit in gardens until they're ready to seed a new world with Imagination and Memory.

Just let them *create* until every molecule returns to the Source.

Let them create *anything*, and from Creation they will eventually remember who they really are, and who they are meant to become. Is it any wonder, *or accident for that matter*, that the CIA secretly and financially backed the most avant-garde artists like Jackson Pollock, and a slew of other fringe musicians, playwrights, poets, and writers of the last century? The CIA fronted dozens of cultural foundations and world exhibits to showcase its most powerful weapon against the Soviet Union's tyrannical rule of conformity, and this weapon was free-expression. And it worked.

But conformity is what Dr. Renn and her colleagues are seeking, is it not? As well as the frustrated loved ones of veteran-patients like the wife of Colonel Condor, stepmother to the boy?

Conform.

Be normal, whatever that is.

Get over it.

Forget what you've done, what you've seen, what you've heard.

Sleep it off.

Don't sleep it off.

Instead, *take–this–pill–then–these–pills–then–record–results–if–you–ever–wake–up.*

No wonder, or accident, Dr. Renn and her colleagues and the many loved ones of the Self-imprisoned-Worthless feel so helpless and rejected. No matter how artfully they gift-wrap Worth, until their recipient accepts the gift, all the well-intentioned gift-packages of Worth in the world are stamped return-to-sender.

What is Worth, anyway? Why do you suppose the Self-imprisoned-Worthless refuse to accept their gifts? What do you suppose they would discover if they were to allow themselves the unwrapping of those gifts?

Inside, they would discover a quantum of Light, Benevolence, and Compassion that spirals all the way back to the Truest Selves and their Source. Picture a dazzling hummingbird-swirl of such energetic brightness and purity to diminish thousands of layers-upon-layers of Guilt and Doubt and Regret. This is why even a single match struck inside the longest cone of tunnel-darkness provides a spark of Light that can be detected from a great distance. We know of your (eventual) coming!

Follow the Light.

We hold the Light.

And so, we also encourage Dr. Renn and the loved ones of her patients like the boy and his stepmother, Sharyn Condor, like Dove Jennings and Harold Jay, to strike and hold their own types of matches and light candles. We encourage them to spread their Benevolent Light from one to another until, hopefully, one day the Dark diminishes long enough for Dr. Renn's Self-imprisoned-Worthless patients like Phoebe and Colonel Condor to reclaim their journeys back to their Light-filled Purpose.

We know how difficult this is for you to accept and allow. We feel your pain, even from the other side of the veil. If Phoebe and Colonel Condor—the boy and his stepmother, and Dove and Jay—could only see how loudly we cheer for them, for all of you, during breakthroughs of Compassion, or how loudly we shout '*No-No, not left—right! Please take a right here!*' We cannot interfere, except in the most extreme circumstances. But we are reaching out to you, Dear Ones, in your dreams, through the visions we send you, through all manner of signals. You happen upon three rare quarters together with the year 1991, and chalk this up to meaningless coincidence. To nature—the birds, bees, insects, turtles, snakes, and other wild things—we whisper requests they deliver, and still most of you sleepwalk by them. Some of you even *try* to run over them with your cars. We do not judge. We try again. We drop feathers at your feet or tuck them in a dresser drawer for future discovery. We send you numbers, hoping to elevate your vibrational remembrance. We send you messages through your computers, through your televisions, through your telephones and other electronic devices. We send our bravest, most compassionate to walk among you. We're the Voice in your head that causes you to look over a shoulder for another source. We're the sudden breeze that tickles the fine hairs of your forearm.

We are you!

All this we do because we love you, because we want you to know that you are never alone, and because you are carrying within you a special purpose—*your* incredibly important part that must be played in the beautiful Game of Humanity. So, we wish to say to you in this moment—

Wake up!

Remember who you are, Magnificent Powerful One, and why you are truly here!

Remember old George Plover, deceased poet laureate of the Cooper VA? George woke up one day, or eventually remembered. It was the day his Army-major grandson, an Iraq veteran, parked his truck across the railroad path of an oncoming train in Germany. This *coincidence* of his grandson taking his own life in the very country where George had taken the lives of so many Germans finally jolted George awake. His grandson had chosen suicide as an exit strategy, despite our signaling against this. The grandson's suicide could have been accomplished in any number of ways, but in his choosing to exit in *Germany,* the grandson gifted the grandfather with an Awakening in George's eighty-first year. George could have chosen to remain in the Dark. No one would have blamed him after witnessing the Darkest of Humanity there during the Battle of the Bulge, but after the Awakening, George began pouring his grief into poetry. From this came a spark. And then a connection. George connected the dots, and followed the Light.

This was George's choice of free will too, of course. Everyone has free will. George could have chosen otherwise, and many would have understood. Many would have used him as another type of example—one for the Dark, or just another statistical measurement to perpetuate their concept of helpless-hopeless small thinking. But George chose otherwise. However bad Harold Jay might claim George's poetry to be because it lacked rhyme and meter, George discovered a poetic-connection to his expanded Self. He provided a Light example for Dr. Renn and her colleagues. Is it any wonder then they exposed poor George to a litany of tests—blood tests and brain scans—so desperate are they, all of you, for a quick cure?

YOU are the cure.

George cured himself.

His body quit when George was ready to lay the body aside. Dove and Jay knew this by the layout of George's home the afternoon they made that welfare check. While they waited for the funeral home, they sat on either side of George's bed and thanked their friend. They recalled his earliest storytelling attempts through poetry that he'd begun sharing with those in the smoking circles on the patio of the Cooper VA. George's bravery, or his poems—they were never sure which—shed a light-filled way back to Worth for Dove Jennings and Harold Jay and so many others who gathered around to listen. After all, George had survived brutal combat and wintery conditions too, only his weren't in Korea like Dove's and Jay's. George's had been in the Ardennes during the Battle of the Bulge.

Plover's poems could produce striking images, such as the images of George and his fellow soldiers of the 101st wrapping their feet in whatever drapes or newspapers they'd find from bombed-out homes along the sixty-mile Patton-push-pull against the Nazis. The poetic lines revealed how affected George had been by the general's shout to, *Lead, follow, or get out of the way.* Despite how hard Dark worked toward victory over George Plover's soul, George appeared to work ever harder—determined to lead with Light, follow Light, or to simply get out of his own way. For years since his grandson's suicide, George held the Light for Dove Jennings and Harold Jay and many, many others at the Cooper VA, and Dove and Jay have been holding the Light ever since.

Follow the Light.

That evening before lights out on the psych ward, Willis fox-walk-sneaks past the bruiser-orderlies into Phoebe's room to check on her. He expects to find her asleep. Instead, she's sitting upright in a chair in the south corner of the small room, as if she's been waiting on his arrival. A thin white blanket envelops her tiny body and her hair appears whiter than ever. Gray Phoebe radiates Light, and Willis rushes toward the Light and drops to the floor at her feet. "I see you, Hawk," she whispers. "Thank you for coming to me." She slowly withdraws her left hand from under the blanket. Willis detects the rustle of paper, and when she produces the note on her lap, he is surprised and not surprised. Hasn't he anticipated this very moment a hundred, a thousand times since leaving her the note he knew she'd find when she was ready to visit the grave of a boy she had once kissed passionately goodbye just before the lights went out in Pleiku and forever intertwined their Spirits?

"All I have to do is deny you," she whispers. "That's all I've ever had to do, you know? Just deny you and go on. Deny you and they'll let me out of here. I can go home. They'll say I'm cured. They'll throw a party in my honor—their honor, actually—and all I have to do is deny you." Tears are springing forth, and Willis reaches up with a handkerchief to catch each precious tear of near-remembrance.

"Denying me—still doesn't make it true," he whispers.

"But I'm tired of denying you…I don't want to deny you anymore."

As she withdraws her other hand from under the blanket, the note glides to the floor and disappears under the bed across the room. Willis would have retrieved the note, except that Phoebe has pulled him closer. She leans forward to kiss his left cheek and then his right. She kisses the middle of his forehead, and finally, his lips. "I was your last kiss…." she says, and leans back. Her eyes flutter and close and leak.

"And my first since…." he says, and pats her face with his handkerchief. Realizing her night medication has won over for the moment, he lifts her from the chair and carries her to the bed, each shoe dropping with a soft thud to the floor. At the bed, he adjusts the pillow for her and brushes aside the long white hair that has fallen across and affixed to her damp, beautiful face. The white blanket appears too thin for protection, even over the voluminous gray jumpsuit, and so he reaches for the blanket folded at the foot of the bed and tucks her in. Just before leaving, he gathers her shoes and places them, toes facing out, under the bed. He remembers the note. Should he retrieve it? If he doesn't retrieve it, will she find it again? Does she need to? Does someone else need to? He takes a deep breath to surrender and swims toward the Nothingness for an answer.

A moment later, Willis departs from Phoebe's room, and the soft click of the door lock falls hard against his heart.

CHAPTER 10

JULY 2 falls on a Thursday, and Willis knows the boy and his father will soon arrive at the Cooper VA. For some reason unclear to Willis at this time, the stepmother will not be joining them. Perhaps he would know the reason if he weren't so distracted with preparations for the boy's arrival. One of the preparations calls for Willis to step outside long enough to explain to the hawk why the biscuits won't be forthcoming from the boy today, and why they won't be forthcoming until late afternoon after the caring for the hummingbirds. The hawk circling overhead, ever benevolent, appears to understand and flies off.

Another preparation for the boy's visit today calls for Willis to wait with a golf cart at the picnic table closest to the cemetery entrance. A heat wave has settled into the valley, and Teana Martin was complaining earlier while filling containers of lemonade and water for him and the boy and packing sandwiches and brownies that she stored in a cooler with gel packs about it being hot enough outside to fry an egg and much too hot for what Willis and the boy will be doing during the hottest part of the day.

"Can't be helped," he said.

"You could wait until closer to sunset," she said. "Why you didn't do this at sunset last night…get somebody to help you instead of waiting on that boy." She means well. "Suppose he don't even come today." Teana Martin is a young soul with an ever-expanding heart.

Willis waits at the picnic table under the shade of still junipers and pines, and in the beauty of his own stillness he reaches the boy in the Nothingness. Soon, the boy emerges from the exit door of the north tower and waves. Instead of dodging the jerky path of sprinklers, he runs into them, dances a quick circle with his arms overhead in victory, and laughs. Who can help but love the boy that still lives within the boy?

Today the boy is dressed in khaki shorts and a T-shirt the indigo shade of deep ocean. The khaki shorts reveal the splash pattern of the sprinkler, but the drops have been absorbed by the ocean-shirt. "Do you know how to drive that thing?" the boy says, smiling—until he sees what's in the back of the golf cart. "Oh…."

"Got a real job to do today. Hoping you'll give me a hand."

"What about the hawk?" the boy says and steps from the shadow of the juniper shade to search for the hawk.

"Done told him about this. He's real sorry he'll miss you today."

The boy shrugs and walks toward the golf cart. "Let's get it over with. But I'm driving."

Under Willis's instruction the boy steers them, too fast, between the stone columned entrance of the cemetery.

While neither speaks, both are surely enjoying the breeze of this long drive past row after row of white headstones. Nearing the office of the cemetery groundskeeper they pass another golf cart that has been parked half on grass, half on pavement, and Dove Jennings and Harold Jay, who are working their rows, pause to wave.

"Semper Fi!" shouts Dove as he limps to the next grave.

Jay hollers, "Oohrah!"

And the boy throws up a hand but continues on up the steep hill, and then around the curve at the top that provides a backward glimpse over the treetops of the north tower's barred windows where perhaps Phoebe, Willis likes to imagine, sits and watches. And then the boy drives all the way to the farthest point of the cemetery where he will park at the row where Phoebe located the note at the grave of a boy she kissed goodbye in Vietnam just before lights-out.

"This will take forever, you know," the boy says, after parking the golf cart, and roughly scooping together an armful of small American flags. Several flags drop to the ground and he crushes them underfoot. Willis feels the tug at his heart, but this too he must accept and allow. The boy huffs toward the final row of graves and jabs a flag into the earth. Willis attends to the graves of another row but looks up frequently to observe the boy's actions. The boy, however, never looks up. He doesn't want to read the names on grave stones. Reading them would be too close to acknowledging them, and this he will not allow himself to do. With spiteful, mindful retribution, the boy stabs the heart of every serviceman and servicewoman with flag after flag.

How many flags and graves will it take?

As many as necessary.

"This sucks, you know!" the boy says, heading back to the golf cart for another armful. He is hot, his face red and sweating, and he pulls up the bottom of the blue-ocean T-shirt to wipe his face. He will pretend not to see the fallen flags on the ground, the ones he crushed and soiled with his footprints, and walks over them every chance he gets as he heads back to plant flags on a second row of graves.

These crushed and soiled flags Willis will have to retrieve, and when he does on his first trip back to the golf cart for more flags, he rolls the fallen ones gently around their wooden masts and places them inside a compartment of the golf cart. In two days, the cemetery will be crawling with family members who deserve far more than finding a soiled American flag at the grave of their loved ones.

Because of the boy's Anger, the job is speeding along. He hasn't spoken in some time, so when they reach the summit of the first hill—the one that allows that view of the barred windows of the north tower—Willis tells the boy to park the golf cart in the shade at the end of one of the rows. The boy complies by jerking the wheel into a left turn that forces Willis to reach overhead with his right hand to secure himself from falling out of the cart. The old Willis—or rather the younger Willis—would have chided the boy and ruined the lessons to come. This Willis knows better, so he accepts and allows the boy to express his Frustration in a way Willis knows the father never would.

The boy shoves hard on the brake pedal, and the cart comes to a near violent stop in front of a large oak. "Now what?"

Willis says nothing as he climbs out of the golf cart. He opens the cooler and hands the boy a boxed lunch prepared by Teana Martin and pours lemonade into plastic cups.

The boy downs the lemonade in a single gulp. Willis pours another. The boy opens his boxed lunch and like a suspicious Caesar examines its contents. "What is this?" he says, holding up the sandwich.

"Are you afraid to find out yourself?"

The boy sighs. After he peels away the plastic wrap, he lifts one slice of bread and sniffs. "Turkey, I guess." He balances the sandwich on his right leg and reaches back into the box. This time he's holding one of Teana Martin's famous brownies. "All right!" he says, and this time hurries through the layers of plastic, but when the prize is revealed he stops. "Guess I'm supposed to eat the sandwich first, huh?"

Willis glances around the cemetery for effect. "See anyone here who cares what order you eat your lunch?"

The boy appears stunned at first, and then grasps the meaning and laughs. "True!" But he looks down at the sandwich and back to the brownie in his left hand and wrestles with the decision. Finally, he half-wraps the brownie and sets it back inside the box and starts on the turkey sandwich. After two large bites, the boy looks over at Willis who has been standing outside the golf cart and staring toward the hospital, and through a mouthful of exposed turkey, bread, and mayo says, "Where's yours?"

"I'll eat when the work's done," Willis says.

The boy shrugs and wolfs down the rest of his sandwich that he washes down with the lemonade. The wad of plastic wrapping gets tossed inside the box. The box gets slowly closed, and the brownie gets abandoned. All this Willis notices—what the boy continues to deny and how the boy continues to punish himself because of the Hate he feels for his father.

"Let's get this over with," the boy says, and chucks the box onto the heap of flags in the back of the golf cart. But when he looks over, Willis is moving slowly between the graves with unusual, exaggerated movements that cause the boy to laugh out loud. "What are you doing? Is that the old-man's version of Tai Chi?" But Willis ignores the boy's taunt and continues, moving slowly and deliberately in the spaces between the graves. He makes a full, slow turn and begins the movement back to the boy in the cart. "What the hell?" the boy mutters. When Willis reaches the golf cart, the boy says, "That looks certifiable, you know. They have a floor at the top of Cooper for people who do things like that."

"What you know about that floor?" Willis says, holding onto the top side of the golf cart cover and leaning inward.

The boy shrugs. "My father was up there for a while. A few days."

"Yeah? How you feel about that?"

"How did *I* feel?" The boy snorts. "I was glad he was there, but he didn't feel that way. Told my stepmom he'd kill himself before he ever went back."

"Do you ever talk to him about how he's feeling?"

"Hell no," he says. "I try not to talk to him any more than I have to. Wish my stepmom would get that. She sets him off all the time. She's the problem. Well, she's not *the* problem, *he's* the problem, but she sure doesn't help. Seems she *wants* to trigger—"

Willis fills in the blank for the boy. "Charlie?"

"Yeah, how did you know?"

"I'm sure you mentioned it before. What does Charlie look like?"

The boy rolls his eyes. He lifts the bottom of the indigo T-shirt and wipes the sweat from his face. "Yesterday, my stepmom's in the kitchen, playing back a phone message on the house phone. She has it on speaker—like you'd think she'd know better, right? And my dad's in the living room, watching the news, which is bad enough of a trigger because anything said about over there can set him off, but he overhears the voice mail message and jumps off the couch and storms toward the kitchen, all the way screaming, '*Who the fuck is that? Who the fuck is talking to my wife that way?*'" The boy stares ahead, unaware evidently of the tears that are beginning to splatter like the sprinkler drops against his khaki shorts. "So, he goes screaming into the kitchen with one '*fuck*' after another, and when he gets there the answering machine message is still screaming back with '*fuck this and fuck that*' and my dad screams again, '*Who's talking to you like that? I'll fuck him up!*' and my stepmom yells back, 'That's *Charlie*—that's *you* on the message, Chris!'" The boy finally blinks and tears squirt in four directions. He shakes his head. "Why couldn't I get a normal dad? I wish he hadn't even come home. I wish he'd just go back. That's what he really wants anyway. He's sick, you know? He'd rather be over there dropping bombs on mothers and little kids instead of—"

"Do you really think that's the reason he wants to go back?"

"Why would anyone want to go back? I just don't get it."

But he will get it one day, Willis thinks, as soon as he awakes with the Remembering. He'll remember other lifetimes during which he, too, was the warrior, and fighting for a cause he believed in, and fighting with, and for, those on either side of him. This won't be the last time, either, that this boy summons the warrior, or the last time he'll allow Anger a victory over

Compassion and Love. He'll awake with memory sooner than most because this is his Destiny as an old soul, but even old souls have free choice. Willis is here, he supposes, to help this boy wake sooner, rather than later. He is here so that one day soon, this boy will recall the lifetimes during which men were ruled by unchecked authoritarianism, and their only choice was to either face death on the battlefield or death for refusal to fight in battle. He'll recall the lifetimes during which battle was considered an important rite of passage for a man. And he'll even recall the lifetime during which he was a woman who roared in favor of war and lost sons and a husband and her life swinging a sword against a crusader.

All these memories the boy, and Willis and Phoebe, and Dr. Renn, and Dove Jennings and Harold Jay, and every veteran-patient at the Cooper VA and beyond carry within every cell of their bodies so that when fully activated in quantum time, they will begin to facilitate the new energy. The new energy will lead to a higher collective consciousness. The higher collective consciousness will eliminate war *forever* as the old dark energy for which there will no longer be a home here.

Is it any wonder, then, the boy is suspicious of authority? Is it any wonder the boy questions all authority? Even Willis's authority? Is it any wonder Willis has been chosen to steer this Knowing boy's anger toward his path of Higher Purpose?

Embrace the learning, Eli.

Accept your gifts.

After a few heartbeats of silence, Willis taps the boy's shoulder with the warm steel of his left hand. "Want to learn the fox-walk?" When he has the boy's attention, Willis repeats the exaggerated movements the boy had earlier teased him over.

The boy laughs. "Is that what you call it? No thanks."

"Go ahead and laugh," Willis says, while stealthily fox-walking around a headstone, "but this saved my life more than once in 'Nam."

"Because they figured you for crazy and didn't bother wasting bullets?"

Willis suddenly stops. He folds to his knees and lets out a belly laugh that Dove Jennings and Harold Jay over the next hill can probably hear, maybe even Phoebe locked up high in the north tower. Then, "Get over here," Willis says to the boy, through more laughter.

The boy reluctantly climbs out of the golf cart and walks over, both hands inside the pockets of his shorts. Willis explains that he learned the fox-walk from his grandfather before they left the reservation. The boy interrupts—*What happened to your parents? Is your grandfather still living? Why did your family leave the reservation for Cooper—I didn't think you were allowed to leave? Why don't you have any family? Aren't you ever lonely?*

Willis supplies the briefest, least painful answers, least likely answers to draw more questions, because this story and this journey are not about him, and soon he is able to return the boy's attention to the fox-walk, explaining that when done correctly, the fox-walk slows one's heartbeat, allowing one to regain a sense of calmness and a clearer perspective and awareness about one's surroundings.

"Clearer perspective for what?" the boy says, his fingers wiggling of nervous energy inside those khaki shorts pockets.

"Like maybe why you think your father would prefer to leave you and your stepmother to drop bombs on women and children?"

The boy's eyes dart around the cemetery as if he's expecting *Charlie* to jump from behind a headstone. "Shouldn't we be asking him that?"

The boy, Willis knows, has entered this lifetime with the highest level of future potential reasoning that needs only the correct activation at the correct time. The boy has been the warrior, just as *everyone* has been the warrior at some point in their many lives, and this the boy remembers though he doesn't yet know what he is remembering. He is choking on sanctimony. He's yet to connect, or he's purposely unaware, that several months ago when his father angered him during one of Dr. Renn's sessions, he summoned his ancient warrior-self to slay a harmless black snake. The snake, powerful symbol of transmutation—and the boy killed his own power, even severing this awakening power symbol at the head, no less. But Willis can't tell the boy all of this, of course. The boy isn't ready to hear or know what he isn't ready to accept. So, Willis just taps the side of his head with his steel left hook. "Let's worry about the snakes roaming around in *your* head for now, OK?"

Willis begins his demonstration of the fox-walk. First his right leg moves upward with deliberation, leading with the knee, and then he slowly leans forward so that the right foot gently touches ground, the outer foot first, rolling inward on the ball of the foot so that the heel is last to make contact with the ground. He pauses. Waits.

"What are you waiting for?" the boy says.

"I'm listening."

"To what?"

"Can't you hear it?" Willis still hasn't moved. Not his head, not his eyes. "Shh…." He can feel the boy's rising impatience. The boy is here for the Knowing, and hungers for Knowledge. When Willis senses the right moment, he whispers, "I'm listening to the heartbeat of Mother Earth." And then up comes his left leg with the same deliberate move led by his left knee and followed by the gentle, deliberate placement of the left foot.

Do no harm.

The moment is punctured by the boy's laugh. "You really think that's how a fox walks?"

Willis pivots to face the boy, and as the right knee slowly rises, says, "How many foxes you seen in your lifetime?"

The boy rolls his eyes. "None, I guess. But I'm pretty sure that's not how a fox walks."

"Why you always got to get in your own way? I'm trying to teach you something here."

"OK-OK," the boy says, and feigns a mimicking of Willis's fox-walk.

"Slower," says the Master. "The fox-walk should be like a *prayer*—a prayer upon the ground to honor our Earth Mother."

The boy shrugs and gives it another try. Right knee comes up, and he glides forward. But when his heel touches ground first, Willis offers gentle correction. *Heel last.* The boy's left knee comes up, and his left foot touches ground. Right leg up—and right foot down. Willis notes the boy's steady balance. Left knee up again—

Willis detects a treble of what's to come. The trebling note creates a vibrational resonance that causes Willis to hold his breath. He can't be certain he's right until the boy's right foot touches down, so Willis studies the energetic field of movement around the boy's rising right leg, and when the boy's right foot rolls inward and his heel reconnects with ground, Willis's face broadens into a wide smile.

We live in such a miraculous world!

The boy must sense an internal shifting too, because he now crouches ever-so-slightly like the patient hunter of the fox, like the Dear Ancient One whose blueprint-coded message still resonates within him, reminding him of a time when he first learned how to move in harmonic-rhythm with Earth Mother's heartbeat by walking prayerfully upon her, and of the many ones for whom he taught the fox-walking prayer, and of the many ones who eagerly await his return. And up comes the boy's left knee—gliding forward is his left foot. And this time when his left heel becomes grounded, the boy gasps. He freezes. He is a stop-frame of Remembrance. The boy glances over his shoulder at Willis and smiles with a face full of all-knowing-all-remembering-Light.

The boy must overcome Fear and Doubt.

Willis reaches for an armful of flags and carries them to the still crouching fox-boy who returns to his mission—this time urging, prodding earth and veterans to accept his gifts.

CHAPTER 11

Charlie is coming.

OUTSIDE that hot July afternoon, Willis frees the tiniest ants that have journeyed up the tall metal stands of the hummingbird feeders and into the small openings. He encourages the ants toward the sweet gardenia shrubs in the garden.

In the deep sinks at the back of Teana Martin's kitchen, he washes and dries the glass feeders. He refills each with the cool elixir he keeps stored in one of Teana's refrigerators, and returns to the garden to hang the glass jars filled with what the hummingbirds must surely sense is nectar from the gods. He wonders at times how his sugary concoction compares to the garden's coral bells and morning glories and lantana. Can they tell the difference, he wonders, or is all sweetness the same to hummingbirds, separated only by degrees?

Can you ever have too much sweetness?

The hummingbirds aren't the only dazzling creatures fluttering within Willis's garden, this summer. A softer cloud of monarchs and swallowtails in yellows and blues, and buttery skippers envelop the butterfly bush that is thriving so wildly it might require a judicious pruning during cooler weather. See now why the Mayans believed the souls of dead warriors returned as butterflies? Already the butterfly bush stands as tall as Willis's waist. What he'd carried single-handedly to the garden from the wheelbarrow a few short months ago would now require several hands if the bush had to be relocated. He promises the butterfly-warrior-souls that he'll plant another bush in the spring, maybe a third, if he's still here, and they can invite the others.

This is the garden he created for Phoebe. He glances up at the barred windows of the north tower, ever hopeful. A whir of white passes near the glass, but these days only the orderlies on the psych ward wear white. He remembers a day when all nurses wore white, even in Vietnam, even when Phoebe wore white. One day, he thinks, bowing down to adjust a sprinkler head in the garden, Phoebe will be well enough to visit her garden. She has everything she needs to heal herself. Everybody does, of course. And this is so hard for most to accept, because most have forgotten why they came here in the first place, much less why they would ever want to return. But everyone remembers, in their own time. They all return and swear they'll do better. Some do, but some have only seconds before taking their final breath to surrender. Some take even longer. But it's all OK, because everyone receives the same celebration from those awaiting their return to the other side of the astral veil. *It's hard work over there*, we remind those who are pouting over unrealized expectations. *You were never alone*, we tell them, *We would never abandon you. You are always loved, Dear Ones, and we thank you for accepting such an auspicious undertaking.*

At this moment in the garden, Willis's efforts are being rewarded, not that he'd ever ask for a reward, by the darting, whizzing, and swirling acrobatic feats of these tiny birds that are thrilling the little ones and their parents this afternoon on the other side of the glass in the east cafeteria. So, when Willis's hand begins to tremble, and he senses the coming of the boy in a cloud of the old energy, he cannot help but recall that disturbing afternoon some time ago now when the boy appeared around the corner of the east dining room with the energy of a barbarian recalled from a hundred lifetimes ago, and carrying the lifeless body of a snake.

But how far the boy has come since, Willis reminds himself.

Tell this to his heart with its most powerful vibrational field of energy that is manifesting uneasiness throughout Willis's chest and down the length of his outstretched right arm and hand that is trying to steady the shallow red plastic cup of sugar water for the hummingbirds. Quickly, the hummingbirds sense the change of energy, and suspicion hangs like a net over the garden, for how can they not also associate this vibration with the memory of that day the boy approached with his decapitated victim? The hummingbirds, ever aware as all nature is, of synchronicity, move farther from Willis's hand, and then higher above the garden. Anyone with any awareness at all can detect the disturbing sense to the crystalline grid of harmony that normally vibrates within Willis's garden. Even the parents, intuiting something themselves—because awareness is a pool of collective consciousness they need only wade into for lifesaving, valuable information—are pulling their children from the windows of the east dining room. The children protest with shrieks that penetrate the wall of glass.

A sudden vacuum of sound descends over Willis in the garden.

But several hours later, with a heavy heart of concern for the boy who never showed, Willis is pushing his janitorial cart inside an elevator that he'll take to the psych ward for a visit with Phoebe. He has tucked gardenias and roses from the garden into a makeshift vase on his cart, and the floral scent quickly fills up the elevator.

When the doors open, Willis is assaulted by an anger energy field. In the hallway he pauses for a moment, contemplating a right turn this time instead of a left that will take him to his past with Phoebe. Left—the ward is noisier than usual. Even from here he can see the movement of a handful of others at the end of the long, polished hallway that ends with the nurses' station, the family waiting area, and the locked double doors that open to Phoebe. But even from here he can hear the deep-tone-shouts of Anger and Hate. Most veteran-patients have swallowed their evening medications by now and are fast approaching the comatose condition, which is why Willis would have preferred earlier evening visits with Phoebe. He's doing the best he can, you know. He has to manage so many challenges—slipping past the orderlies is one of the toughest.

For reasons he doesn't yet fully understand, he feels pulled to push his janitorial cart toward this chaos, and as he gets closer, he discovers it's Dr. Renn standing at the nurses' station, conferring with two bruiser-orderlies and the night nurse. Her white doctor's jacket, normally pristine even after a long day's work, has an unkempt appearance, as if she pulled this one at the last minute from a dirty laundry hamper. Even from this distance, Willis identifies that her voice is dry and hoarse, and the bags of puffiness tug on her bottom eyelids. And there's Dove Jennings, sitting slumped in a chair of the family waiting room. Harold Jay stands nearby, practically in the center of the small lobby, and blocking Willis's view of most of the woman who is sitting in the chair behind him. From this angle, Willis can only make out her thin legs and white sneakers, that the legs are crossed at the knee—right over left—and that her right foot is fidgeting. He sees the white cuff of what is probably a pair of white shorts and the outer edges of her yellow blouse.

Dove waves over Jay, and when Jay clears out of the way, Willis sees the whole image of the woman in the chair—and knows in that way that Willis knows that he is facing for the first time the tiny song-stolen canary-wife of Colonel Christopher Condor, and stepmother to the boy.

Willis glances toward the men's restroom. Is the boy there, behind the door?

"How could he be so selfish?" the song-stolen canary blurts out into the lobby, and leaps to her feet as if she's decided to take flight. Everyone has stopped what they're doing. "He's not a child," the woman says, looking around the room for an ally. Dove and Jay say nothing, and look toward Dr. Renn for answers. "He knew what a letter like that would do to his father."

Dr. Renn mutters something undetectable to the night nurse who nods and lifts the phone receiver to place a call. One of the orderlies disappears behind the double doors, and lets spill into the lobby a string of *Charlie* threats laced with *fucks* into the lobby.

"Sharyn, don't leave me in here.

Sharyn, don't fucking leave me in this fucking place.

Sharyn, I'll fucking kill you when I get out of here.

I'll fucking kill every one of you mother fuckers."

Sharyn Condor, eyes wide with fear, grabs a large, brown handbag from the floor. "He'll never forgive me for doing this," she says and bursts in tears. "We've come so far, too, and now this."

The orderly reappears. He holds two small white cups that Dr. Renn carries to the colonel's wife. "We'll need you here a little longer, so this might help." The colonel's wife shakes her head. "Please let us help. We'll be sure you and Eli get home safely. And please know the colonel will be much calmer in a few minutes. What seems ugly now won't be in a day or so."

"He'll never forgive me."

"I know this is hard to believe right now, but Chris won't even remember most of tonight because of the condition he's in. Remember, this could have been so much worse. Let's remember that."

The woman drops the brown handbag in a chair. She takes the cups from Dr. Renn. Before swallowing the pills, she adds, "He did this on purpose, you know. He did this out of spite."

Dr. Renn takes a chair opposite the woman. "Where is he now?"

"How should I know?" the woman says, and when she throws her head back to swallow the pills, Dr. Renn shoots a knowing look at Dove and Jay. Jay helps Dove from the chair and the two men excuse themselves and head toward the elevator.

Of course, nobody's even noticed Willis standing there beside his janitorial cart. He's invisible.

Inside a supply closet behind Teana Martin's kitchen, Willis stashes his janitorial cart. He deadbolts the door from the inside and closes his eyes. After a few deep breaths to surrender, he has found the beautiful Nothingness, and in the Nothingness he searches for the boy. Turns out the boy is searching for him too. A lump rises in Willis's throat. He unlocks the supply closet door and rushes to the exit door in the east dining room that leads to the garden. He pushes open the door and sees the boy running up the hill from the picnic table where they often call for the hawk.

"Willis!" the boy shouts. "I've been looking everywhere for you!"

"Eli, I'm here."

The boy falls into Willis's arms. "I almost killed him. What's wrong with me? I almost killed him, Willis."

"But you didn't. He's fine. I heard him upstairs. Mad as hell, but he's very much alive, and they're taking real good care of him." Willis guides the boy to one of the stone benches in the garden. All is quiet this time of evening. Only the gurgling of the water fountains and the occasional, comical croak of the bullfrog from the retention pond punctuate the stillness. The boy shares that his father had turned into *Charlie* over the weekend, and finally the boy had reached his limit and written a letter to his father.

"I said really bad things too. I told him he was ruining my life, and that I could never be proud of him or anyone like him because I'd never kill someone and expect to get a medal for it." The boy says he left the letter is his father's car and when the father had run to the store, he'd found the letter. "He didn't come home that night, and Sharyn—she was just going crazy. She kept calling his phone and leaving voice mails until finally she couldn't leave any more because his mailbox was full." At some point that first evening, Sharyn Condor had also checked the medicine cabinet and hit the panic button when she realized that Chris had been gone all day without his heart medication that controlled his irregular heartbeat. This was when she'd begun calling family to organize a search.

For the next hour, a steady stream of friends and family poured into the Condor house and the kitchen became the center of operations. Chris's brother, also an Air Force veteran but one who hadn't seen any combat, established a concept of operations—who would do what, who would call whom, who would go where to check. They knew they couldn't count on police authorities to help until Chris had been missing twenty-four hours. That could be too late. Maybe it was already too late.

All this the boy says he watched quietly while leaning against the doorframe that divided the kitchen from the living room. He told no one about the letter he had written and left in the car for his father to find. Besides, what proof did he have anyway that his father was missing because of the letter he had written?

So off they went to cover each cardinal direction of possibility and probability. The boy was left at home with instructions to call if his father showed up or called with his whereabouts. They were gone until early morning. Some time after midnight the boy had fallen asleep on the living room couch, but he jumped to his feet when he heard the chime of the back-door alarm. He raced to the kitchen, hoping to see his dad, ready to face whatever version of his dad might be returning—*Dad or Charlie, just let him be OK.*

Instead, his stepmother, uncle with three boxes of doughnuts in his arms, and the rest of the family-friend search entourage spilled into the kitchen. His stepmother started a pot of coffee. A few hours later, the empty doughnut boxes lay in a pile near the back door. The coffee had been refilled at least twice. One police officer took a statement from the boy's stepmother.

"I just don't know why he'd leave. Everything's been better than ever—sure he gets mad sometimes, but he's never mad at me. He's just mad at life or at other things. You know how it is."

Another police officer was rapidly recording from the boy's uncle the list of locations that had been searched during the night. The officer looked over at the boy. "We'll find him, son," he said. "Any idea where your father might have gone, or maybe what set him off to do this? If we know that, we might have a clue about where he went." That's when the boy came clean, describing his anger and how he'd written his father a letter and left it for him in the car.

The stepmother leaped to her feet and lashed out. "If anything happens to Chris," she said, "it's all your fault." The uncle attempted to restrain her, according to the boy. "You know better than this," the stepmother said. "How selfish can you be? He's your father, for crying out loud. He's made sacrifices you'll never understand. You're *nothing* compared to him. You'll never be anything compared to him."

When the boy finishes telling the story to Willis, he falls silent. The glow of light from the miniature solar lamps

Willis installed weeks earlier in the garden illuminate the boy's sadness. A couple of nurses on a nightshift break push into the garden from the east dining room but are too caught up in a conversation to notice Willis, and they barely acknowledge the boy. After they pass, Willis says, "So your father finally came home?"

The boy shakes his head.

"Where did they find him?"

"I found him, Willis," the boy says. "Sorta…the way you taught me to call for the hawk." The boy explains that after his stepmother's outburst he'd gone to his room and closed the door. He'd remembered how to breathe and how to find the Nothingness, though he doubted for a while that this would really work the way it had worked for the hawk. He says for a moment he even doubted whether he was the one who had ever called for the hawk—that maybe he couldn't find the hawk, or even reach the Nothingness without Willis. But he kept trying. Finally, he found the Nothingness. And in the Nothingness, he saw his father lying under bright lights. The word *hospital* entered the boy's consciousness, and so he ran back to the kitchen and motioning for one of the police officers, explained that he'd seen his father in a hospital room. "The officer looked at me kinda strange," the boy says. But the officer thanked him, and when the uncle, curious about the conversation, walked over, the officer explained the boy's "vision." The boy's uncle started issuing orders for everyone to pick a hospital and to start calling.

The stepmother sat glumly at the kitchen table with a cup of coffee. Finally, someone reported that a John Doe who matched the description of Colonel Christopher Condor had been admitted by ambulance a couple of hours earlier. The family would learn the details later—how officers answered a call about a man wandering the park in a belligerent state of mental confusion, and when they tried to subdue the man, Colonel Christopher *(Charlie)* Condor suffered a mild heart attack.

Before leaving the Condor home, both police officers thanked the boy for his honesty and assistance. "They were just trying to make me feel better," the boy tells Willis. "None of this would have happened if I hadn't written that letter."

What Willis understands and could explain about time would be enormously helpful here, but too confusing for the boy to grasp in this condition of Guilt. The oldest of oldest souls bear the deepest layers of Guilt and Regret from hundreds of lifetimes, and this is why it can take some of them longer than others to awake to their Light and Purpose. The boy, being one of the oldest, and one of the Chosen with a special assignment, has already discovered how much easier it is to default to the older energy, and the consequences. And the boy is not through with the old energy yet. This realization ushers forth a disturbing premonition appearing as a series of flashing still images—there's a vision of Phoebe standing in the garden, her arms outstretched for help. Another vision— death surrounds the boy, too shaken to run for cover from the aerial release of bombs. So many bombs. So much destruction.

Willis can't connect these disturbing visions in a way that will help him alter probabilities to mere potentials, at least not yet, and his entire body produces a shudder.

What degree of difficulty lies among miracles?

Not one.

But this boy possesses the strong probability of defaulting at least once more to the old dark energy, and if Willis will accept and allow this—whatever the personal cost or pain—the probability will this time lead to the boy's greatest Awakening. Does this mean Willis must sacrifice Phoebe for the boy?

What more is being asked of him? *Take another limb*, he thinks. *Take what's left of my soul.* Sitting here with the boy in this flowering Center of Creation, Willis tries to calm the internal shuddering. He reminds himself he is here to help activate the boy, and that all will be revealed in its proper time. One day, perhaps, Willis will sense the proper timing to explain to the boy that time isn't linear at all the way time appears to us in these physical bodies. Time is quantum, and this means the boy was always going to write that letter because past, present, and future are actually happening at the same time. One day, perhaps, Willis will share with the boy how to rewrite his own future, as Willis has done and will attempt, again, to save Phoebe, and maybe help the boy avoid the most painful lesson yet ahead of him. But not today. Not tonight here in the garden with the boy's father upstairs threatening to kill everyone and the boy weighted by Guilt and Regret.

Willis lets out a heavy sigh.

"You're disappointed in me too," the boy says.

Willis wraps his right arm around the boy's shoulders and looks to the stars. "Not my job to judge you, or anyone else for that matter. Besides, all you did was write what you been feeling for a long time. Don't think your father didn't already know how you felt. Folks think they're smarter, more evolved and elegant 'cause they can filter what comes out of their mouths—when it's what's coming out of their minds they need to filter."

The boy pulls away to look up at Willis. "You make it sound like we're all mind-readers. I can't read anyone's mind."

Willis chuckles and roughly pulls the boy close. "Boy— you one of the best mind-readers walking the planet, and don't even know it."

CHAPTER 12

WHAT are a few months locked up as a POW in the Cooper VA psych ward for someone like Phoebe who survived 313 days as a POW in Vietnam? The list of indignities is too great to mention. Whatever you can imagine is probably not harsh enough to make that list.

After she had been missing for six months, her family gave up and held a memorial service so that when she was finally rescued and returned home, she had a pile of bureaucracy to battle through just to reclaim her identity. After all she'd been through, this bureaucratic nightmare felt ever more injurious. A name change would have been far easier. A fresh start seemed most appropriate, given the media attention that elicited inappropriate public discussions about why women had no business anywhere close to the front line of combat. *See? This is what happens when you send a woman to war.* Or, *Remember Phoebe Kennedy...nobody wants to become another Phoebe Kennedy.* And, *The U.S. can never allow another Phoebe Kennedy.* Her own family tiptoed around her. Nobody asked how she was feeling or whether she wanted to talk about anything. Her father, the WWII veteran of the family, was no more help than her mother. During his first week in Europe, he had been accidentally shot in the toe by a fellow soldier who had fallen asleep on post and discharged his weapon. Her father was soon home again with one less toe, a Purple Heart, and a medical discharge.

After she managed to rescind the death certificate and renew her life, she left her parents' home in Pennsylvania for a job at the Cooper VA. One of the doctors recognized her from their time in Pleiku. They'd liked each other even then, an instant chemistry typical between nurses and doctors— even the married ones—who found it easy to justify any sort of behavior when you never knew when or where the next incoming mortar might land. But while Phoebe was just beginning her year of service in country, her doctor-friend was nearing the end of his, so they made the best of the month they had together, and then he was gone. She received one letter from him to say he'd taken a job with the VA, but didn't reveal which VA, and this was revelation enough that he wasn't considering her in his future plans. She forgot him and moved on to another, and another, and another. A string of doctors who came and went—some left for other field evacs with emergency needs, some left in body bags. You kept your sanity best you could while knee-deep in blood, guts, and discarded limbs of young soldiers and Marines.

Imagine Phoebe's surprise when she rediscovered her first Pleiku doctor at the Cooper VA. He appeared equally surprised and more than interested, not to mention long ago divorced, so they rekindled what they thought they'd sparked in Pleiku. All the drinking helped, of course, and soon Phoebe was pregnant. This wasn't her first pregnancy. You can't suffer what Phoebe suffered for 313 days and escape pregnancy. But internment's lack of nutrition, coupled with physical beatings and other physical and emotional stresses, caused her body, or her mind, to reject what it couldn't have sustained in such an environment.

But *this* pregnancy in Cooper, she thought, will be sustainable. She'd put the weight back on, and been treated with so many rounds of antibiotics since her return to the States she'd avoided every influenza outbreak and flu bug for two years. Here in the sleepy, peaceful valley of Cooper ringed by the majesty of blue-purplish mountains—this was a world in which to bring a child. She married the doctor, and they bought a bungalow on the side of a steep hill that overlooked the valley. But during the fourth month, her body objected and rejected this pregnancy too, and four months later, Phoebe rejected her doctor-husband, who sold the bungalow below market for a quick relocation to another VA across country, and didn't tell Phoebe which VA. She could have found out had she really wanted to know, but she didn't. Life—hers anyway—resembled a repeating pattern of disillusionment, and she assumed this meant she was here to conquer disappointment in all its many forms rather than seek any sort of self-fulfillment.

Vowing to avoid as many repeating patterns as possible, Phoebe chose to remain single, despite a number of proposals over the next several decades. She found all the companionship she could handle within the veteran community of the Cooper VA—in her caring of Vietnam veterans especially, and during meaningful conversations with Dove Jennings and Harold Jay who would often encourage her to take an art class or a writing workshop.

"One day," she'd say, never intending to attend. Phoebe had resisted therapy for decades, until the day she found herself sitting in Dr. Renn's office because of the sudden return of nightmares, one in particular involving an Army sniper. Only Phoebe never got around to discussing the nightmares or the sniper that day. She talked, instead, about gardening. "Someday I want to create a garden full of flowers—something teeming with life."

"What's stopping you?" Dr. Renn said. "Why not garden? Or how about *painting* flowers—why not take one of our art classes?"

"It's fine for others to be stimulated by creativity," she said, "but after a day of caring for vets in hospice care, the last thing I want is to be stimulated—by anything, or anyone for that matter."

Dr. Renn pressed her. "But isn't gardening just another form of creativity?"

Phoebe shook her head, explaining that digging up warm soil, discovering the magic of earthworms, and planting seeds sounded as relaxing to her as the idea of a warm bubble bath might sound to others. But Phoebe never got around to planting that garden. She had drawers filled with magazine tear sheets of gardening ideas.

The next time, the last time before Phoebe's *crack*, Dr. Renn pressed her about planting a garden, Phoebe finally admitted, "I just can't decide what to plant—too many choices, too many decisions."

"What are you afraid of?"

"Wasting time, I suppose." A second later, her eyes widened. "*No*—that's not it. I'm afraid of wasting the potential life within each seed. What if I can't cultivate that potential?

The responsibility is too great. I'm not ready." Never mind the scores of near-dead souls Phoebe Kennedy, favorite nurse at the Cooper VA, had coaxed back to life. She couldn't, or wouldn't, make the connection. By the time Willis showed up in Cooper, Phoebe had reached the mindset that life—hers anyway—was just the necessary evil of passing time until you could finally be done with it all, and enter a joyous, blissful, alarm-clock-free, eternal sleep.

Of course, she'd contemplated suicide at least a thousand times. She spent nights in terror of those nightmares. She spent chunks of her day when she wasn't working at the Cooper VA daydreaming about how life might have been had she never volunteered for assignment in Vietnam, or had her child with the doctor-husband lived. Who might she have been had she experienced a *normal* life here in Cooper? Would marriage and motherhood—deemed relatively normal by most—have prevented her from finally cracking so far wide open under the pressure of what she'd been denying for so many years? You see, Phoebe didn't crack open from all that had been done *to* her, as do most.

No one would deny that Lieutenant Phoebe Kennedy, U.S. Army nurse held 313 days in a Vietnamese prison camp, had been a victim of the darkest energy humanity could afflict upon another living soul. But even this wasn't what finally cracked Phoebe Kennedy. What she suffered in that prison camp she accepted as her punishment, and this extraordinary acceptance served her well for years—right up until the day Willis showed up at the Cooper VA.

It's now the third week in August, hot and dry in the valley, and another Thursday. In fact, the boy is coming today to visit his father who is to be released after thirty days of treatment on the psyche ward. During evening visits with Phoebe, Willis saw the colonel three times—the first time the colonel was slumped in a chair near one of the windows in the group room and appeared to be heavily medicated. The other two times, the colonel was sitting at one of the large round tables in the group room, keeping to himself and drawing sketches of other veteran-patients—quite extraordinarily detailed sketches too. Willis saw the colonel hand a sketch to a veteran who had been the unknowing subject of the artist, and the veteran looked curiously at the sketch and said, "Don't know him—ask Smitty over there." Late one evening while emptying the trash, Willis discovered a loosely crumpled ball of paper lying to the left of the trash can as if the sketch-ball had been a missed free-throw. He peeled apart the rough paper, and the sketched faces—quite magnificent ones too—of the boy and the boy's stepmother stared up at him. Actually, the boy's gaze had been drawn with averted, downcast eyes; Sharyn Condor's, a suspicious glance toward the right.

When he folded the sketch in half, intending to keep this fine work for the boy, Willis noticed the writing on the opposite side. Four attempts at a brief poem. Whole lines crossed out, rewritten, re-ordered, and then crossed out again, each an attempt with unmistakable Rumi-mysticism to define a man's internal chaos, and each attempt signifying a more urgent, deep yearning, perhaps even a destined or desperate need to complete this poem. Perhaps the colonel suspected what we've been telling you all along—that he was creating his own reality. Willis studied the lines again, the cross-outs and the do-overs, and pulling a pen from his shirt pocket, conscribed a clean version of the colonel's last attempt to the right side of the page. Willis changed nothing. But he did add one word.

Desire.

And then he turned the paper over, allowing the faces of the boy and his stepmother to greet the colonel in the morning, while he went back to his job of emptying the trash and scraping pain-graffiti from the walls.

Willis may have only seen the colonel three times, but he's passed the colonel's wife in the hallways and shared elevator rides with her nearly every one of those thirty days. She never noticed Willis, but make no mistake about it—Sharyn Condor has become the Cooper VA model of medical advocacy for her husband. On the morning of the colonel's release, she rode the elevator to that sixteenth floor with two nurses and sang all the way to sixteen like a tiny wren who's just discovered she's the most powerful voice in the forest.

The colonel must have been ready for release because Willis certainly knows Dr. Renn could have manufactured a dozen reasons of preventing Colonel Condor's release—just look how long she's kept Phoebe locked up. Willis attributes the colonel's release to a good sign, and today he's looking forward to the boy's report—hoping his report will hint at a healing, or at least an understanding between father and son.

While the boy's father was undergoing his thirty days of treatment, the boy and Willis shared a number of experiences each Thursday. They discussed constellations and galaxies and astral physics and the energy in rocks—the energy in everything, frankly. The boy earned the trust of the hawk that now perches atop the boy's shoulder before or after the biscuit offering. Since the father's lock-up in Cooper, the boy has been living nearby with his uncle, and the uncle has been seeing to it that the boy attends his regularly scheduled therapy sessions with Dr. Renn. But the uncle appreciates even more the boy's newfound interest in helping the Cooper VA maintenance department, so the uncle drops the boy off several hours earlier than the appointment time, and with plenty of money for lunch and an afternoon snack.

Treating Colonel Condor during this thirty-day window requires treatment of the whole family. Part of this family treatment calls for the boy to write an essay about his summer, hoping, Willis imagines, that the boy will finally express his guilt or regret or lessons-learned regarding the letter he wrote his father. According to the boy, Dr. Renn continues to pressure him to discuss the emotions leading up to and after the letter-writing episode.

"They have the letter," he says to Willis one Thursday, "so why should I tell them what was in it as if nobody knows? It's asinine-bullshit." Willis silently agrees, but he knows Dr. Renn is doing the best she can to draw out the boy's anger so that she can help him find more appropriate ways with which to respond the next time Anger shows up—for there will be a next time.

While he waits this Thursday on the boy's arrival, Willis pulls weeds in Phoebe's garden and allows his mind to wonder about all the boy might choose to share in a summer essay for his therapy group. Will he write about the hawk? Will he write about the gentle caring each week for the hummingbirds or about tending Phoebe's garden? Will he share about learning the fox-walk among the graves or about discovering the aura surrounding trees or about the power of serpent energy that must always be respected? Will he write about finding feathers in the strangest places where no birds have ever been, and about pondering the symbolism, or about valuing the life of a lizard the same as he would value the life of the hawk, or the life of his father? Will he explain the importance of asking questions and listening in the still Nothingness for the answers? Will he share how he's learned to ask the sacred questions passed down by all the indigenous ones, *What does this mean?* and *What am I missing?* All these things Willis imagines the boy will *want* to write about, if he feels safe enough to share them with his father and the therapy group led by Dr. Renn. And who could be safer than Dr. Renn?

Today, the boy is later than usual, but Willis senses nothing out of sorts. The boy will likely join him in the kitchen when it is time to wash and refill the hummingbird feeders. With a half-hour left before the public hummingbird feeding, Willis uses the time to replace two cracked sprinkler heads run over recently by the grounds crew—whatever good the sprinklers will do for the lawn these days. Thanks to watering and electricity cutbacks, the lawn has been condemned to death. VA administrators think nothing of spending millions on artwork for the hospital when they could be financially supporting veteran-artists, many of whom are actually locked upstairs in the north tower or locked within the stories of their minds as they wander the parks and streets of Cooper, drawing murals with the sharp edges of rocks on the walls of bridge overpasses, sidewalks, and the sides of buildings. They stand on street corners and recite their poetry, or sing, or play guitars for coins or just for the love of stringing together vibrational notes.

Rarely is Willis so caught up in his head that he resorts to judgment, or loses present awareness. But it happens to even the most aware at times, and it happens to Willis on this Thursday afternoon, beginning with the blur of white that finally catches his attention.

How long has she been sitting down there at the picnic table? At first, Willis can't even believe what he's seeing. It's Phoebe. She's wearing white—not nursing whites, but a long column of white dress with bell-shaped sleeves. Can it really be? His Phoebe in white, sitting outdoors at the picnic table that Willis shares with the boy and the hawk? He must show her the garden, he thinks. She must see how he's created and tended the garden in her honor. She will join him and the boy, and the three of them together will feed the hummingbirds. He runs across the lawn, running toward the white vision of Compassion and Love.

Outdoors like this, she appears years younger than she did at the top of the north tower. "I have so much to show you," he says, and climbs over and onto the bench opposite her. "Whatever you had to do or say to Dr. Renn, Phoebe, it doesn't matter. You see that now, right? *You* know the truth. *We* know the truth." He can hardly catch his breath from the run and the excitement.

Phoebe reaches for something on the bench beside her and places it on the table between them. Willis knows without looking what Phoebe has placed between them. "Please don't do this, Phoebe," he whispers. "*Why?* Why would you do this now?"

She places both hands on top of his right hand. "All this time you've been extending what I wasn't ready to extend myself—forgiveness and compassion—"

Willis interrupts, "You did what any compassionate nurse would have done."

In a corner of his mind a spark of Light appears. He intends to ignore it—*deny* the spark of Light the same way Phoebe has been ignoring hers all these years. They don't have to be in the atrium-jungle for him to recognize the sounds beginning to emanate from the dark corners of Memory— the corners that hold the memories of approaching VC and the acrid odor of gunfire that's filling up the Pleiku field hospital ward and the fear and screams for help on the face of the paralyzed soldier strapped into the Stryker just a few feet from Willis, who lies helpless, too, after having lost his left arm. Until *she* appears like a white hovering angel above him, and for a moment she blocks out the fear and the screams of the paralyzed one in the Stryker.

They're coming for me, he whispers. *I'm the sniper.*

I know, Hawk.

Do you understand what I'm asking?

She nods, and leans over. She smells of soap, and roses and gardenias, alcohol and blood, life and death and everything else he longs to spend another lifetime remembering.

Please forgive me, she whispers and presses her mouth hard on his—just as the doors to the field evac hospital burst open.

Willis smiles. "You were my last kiss."

She smiles, and her refreshed, dazzling Light begins the recalibration of every cell in his body. As a flood of new awareness and energy surges through him, every needle on the row of long-leaf pines behind her waves and dances for him. Above this copse of trees, the patch of blue sky and white-capped clouds appear illusory, and he's almost tempted to reach out, push through, and grab hold of the hand awaiting his on the other side. But right now, he's content to hold Phoebe's warm hand. He's waited a long time for this moment. He's waited what some would consider a thousand lifetimes.

"The day I walked out of that POW camp, I decided I was walking out for the both of us," she says, and squeezes his hand.

"We both know what they would have done to me."

"Worse than 313 days? Tell me, is anyone up there really keeping score?"

They sit in silence for a few moments. Twice a breeze lifts the white bell-shaped sleeves of her gown, accentuating her ethereal essence. Finally, "You made me a better nurse," she says. "I tried to deny you, but you were behind the eyes of every soldier who had ever been there. So, I made sure they knew I could see them. When they began to slip away from here, I'd whisper to them, '*I see you.*'" She places her right hand over her heart. "I see *you*, Hawk. I have always carried you here."

When she looks down at the paper between them, Willis says, "Why did you keep this?"

"It wasn't easy," she says, "but I think I always knew this day would come. I guess that's why I finally had this translated years ago by the Vietnamese wife of one of my Army patients." She slides the all-too-familiar letter with the Vietnamese lettering toward Willis. "You've forgiven me. Now it's *your* turn, Hawk," she says. "Take all the time you need."

Don't we teach what we most need to learn?

She leans over the round picnic table, and a sleeve catches for a second on a splinter that seems to know better by its offer of an immediate release. An aura of roses and gardenias envelops him, and he joins her in that halfway space. "When you're ready," she whispers, softly pressing her mouth on his, and afterward, "I'll be waiting in the garden."

What about the boy?

Willis *has* forgotten about the boy for the first time since the boy's arrival to the Cooper VA months earlier. Even now as thoughts of the boy attempt to drive with the same recklessness as the boy's golf cart antics toward the center of Willis's attention, Willis is for the first time pushing back. *For a moment*, he thinks, *just let me think for a moment about what all this is supposed to mean.*

What am I missing?

Sometime later he is still wandering far past the cemetery and deep into the woods on the southernmost outskirts of the hospital's campus. One day, the way it's going now, these woods will be torn from their roots to make room for more of Cooper's finest and bravest dead. The boy is right to question everything. His own ancient records tell him to wonder whether the world will put an end to war, or whether war will put an end to the world.

In the forest, Willis comes upon several trees that have fallen and lay now across each other. He settles into the intersection and recalls stories from Grandfather White Feather about the ancient ones who crawled inside giant trees like these and used their vibrational energies as meditative rockets for traveling the cosmos. Grandfather had promised to show him how one day, but that day never came.

Willis turns his attention back to the letter he'd taken from the dead body of the first-and-only North Vietnamese soldier Willis had been forced to kill in close combat. The young Viet Cong soldier had the misfortune of being on guard duty that evening when he stumbled, literally, over Willis whose reputation for concealment and confirmed kills had already reached legendary status. So concealed was Willis that evening that the young Viet Cong soldier, distracted by this letter he was reading, tripped hard and lost his weapon that landed atop a bush, thankfully not discharging and drawing the attention of the others. When the Viet Cong soldier realized the cause of his stumbling was over the famous U.S. Army sniper, he opened his mouth to send the alarm, and this was the last act of bravery the Viet Cong soldier ever made—in this lifetime.

For some reason, Willis had felt compelled to save the dead soldier's letter. He planned to read it one day, probably Stateside when home safe, drinking a beer—maybe not. Maybe he'd never read the letter. Maybe he shouldn't. But he safeguarded the letter all those months later by keeping it wrapped within a plastic bag that he shoved in a pocket of his trousers. He thought about the letter often. He'd pull it out of the bag and stare at the strange, architectural-styled gibberish, and then fold and return the letter to the plastic bag. Sometimes to keep himself awake so he wouldn't have to relive the nightmares that started after killing the Viet Cong soldier, he'd allow his mind to imagine the letter contained all sorts of military-boring details. Where his unit was going next. A brag about how many U.S. soldiers they'd captured that day. What he didn't want to imagine was that there was anything intimate or loving or...*human* about the letter. He didn't want evidentiary proof of the soldier's soul, if that makes sense. Bad enough this soldier, the only hand-to-hand combat kill for Willis, haunted his dreams during snatches of sleep in the jungle, because during those dreams, the young VC sneaks up behind Willis, drops his saber—severing Willis's left hand, the letter still firmly gripped between fingers that had reflexively tightened their grip against the sight of a swiftly dropping sword. In most dreams, the Viet Cong soldier reaches down and reclaims his letter.

Some nights, the soldier even slices Willis's throat.

But now, decades later, Willis is reunited with the letter. He holds it firmly in his right hand. Vietnamese lettering, though unreadable, still appears as familiar to him now as it did all those years ago. He turns the letter sideways to read what Phoebe's translator has provided in English:

I received your letter when the sun was slowly setting in the East. I got your letter which flew to my hand from a distant place. At that time I was dreaming and remembering the day we first met, and that's when I received your letter.

Anh—when I got your letter, I quickly grabbed a pen and paper to write a few lines on this small piece of paper so that we can talk to each other again about the time we met and knew each the first time. When I hold this pen to write to you in this first letter, I would like to ask about your health. The moon tonight is very bright, how can I forget your images, they still appear in front of my eyes, remembering when we parted—2 people, one South the other one, North. How can I say all the meanings with you at that time? People say "Far away from each other, one will climb a hundred mountains, cross a hundred rivers and pass a thousand hills", so when I didn't receive your letter I said to myself what's the chance I will ever get a letter? And now I have received this letter from you. Please, please write back right away. I am waiting.

Thinh

For a moment, Willis sits in silence, staring at a column of large ants marching along a dead limb of the fallen tree, his head filling with the expressions of poetic hopefulness for a Viet Cong soldier whose voice Willis silenced with a knife. In his mind, Willis hears over and over, *I am waiting, I am waiting, I am waiting.*

What do you imagine happens to a man when he finally faces the truth about the Divinity within his enemy?

As the forest fills with moans and wails, the cicadas and the birds and the ants and all the creatures within the forest bow to the Divinity within a man named Willis.

The boy! The boy!

Willis returns mentally from the jungles of Vietnam to Cooper, remembering again that it's Thursday. He's not sure how long he's been wandering through these woods, but he's far enough now from the cemetery that he can hear the whizzing of trucks and cars on the four-lane that leads into the city. He tucks the letter in a pocket, and starts the journey back to the Cooper VA, back to the boy.

At the top of the cemetery hill, he reaches the vantage point that permits him a view of the north tower. Without Phoebe's presence there, the tower appears even darker than usual. A golf cart, driven by a security guard, is approaching but less than fifty yards from Willis, the driver veers down a long military-precise row of headstones. Riding in the cart are also Dove Jennings and Harold Jay with a woman Willis has never seen before. No one in the cart has ever seen Willis, for that matter. The golf cart comes to a stop at a mound of freshly-moved earth, and Dove and Jay help the woman from the cart over to the new grave.

When he's another hundred yards or so closer to the hospital, Willis detects a calling from the boy. He stops to listen. Something in the boy's tone causes a lump to form in Willis's throat.

What does it mean? What am I missing?

He turns left and runs diagonally between headstones, shortcutting through the woods, passing the gravesite where he and the boy buried the head of the snake. When he reaches the edge of the woods, he stops to catch his breath, but up the hill toward the east dining room he sees the boy. The boy is jumping and running wildly in circles within the garden. The hawk is there too.

"Willis!" shouts Teana Martin who has emerged from the wide loading dock door that backs up to her kitchen. She waves to him, and then runs down the steep steps to the lawn of the hospital. "Hurry, please hurry," she is shouting. Willis meets her halfway, and she is breathless.

"Is it the boy?" he says. "Is he OK?"

She clutches her heart while trying to catch her breath. "He won't be after you're done with him! It's horrible, Willis. I never seen a child that wicked-mad in all my life. He's gone *crazy.* I was out for my new tires, and he come in without you and left a mess in my kitchen. A mess! Dumped sugar everywhere. Tore open I bet a thousand packets of my artificial sweetener—I don't have a clue why." She grabs hold of Willis's right forearm with a strength that surprises, yet doesn't fully surprise him. It's her warmth, the way it's sinking so quickly through skin and already tapping veins that most surprises him. She gives his arm the sort of hard shake you'd use to awaken someone who's slept through an alarm. "Willis—you don't think he's trying to *kill* those poor little birds, do you?

And we been so kind to that boy. You, especially. And he done scared all those kids away from the dining room too, Willis. The parents called security. You have to hurry, Willis!" Poor Teana Martin just can't stop chirping long enough for Willis to focus his thoughts on the boy. What is he missing? Has *Charlie* reemerged and summoned the warrior within the boy?

Just then, the boy stops his wild circling and looks down the hill. As he storms toward Willis and Teana, he shouts, "Where the hell you been? I've been looking everywhere for you." Willis urges Teana to fetch Dr. Renn. Teana finally releases her vice-grip on Willis's arm and runs back up the hill toward the loading dock steps.

"I'm here," Willis calls back, walking up the hill toward the boy. "What's wrong? What's happened?"

Overhead all this time the hawk has been circling and screeching so loudly that Willis is straining to hear and make sense of what's happening. The boy stops to shake his fist at the hawk. "You shut up. I've had enough of you today."

By the time Willis and the boy reach one another, the boy is a wild-eyed wounded animal ready to strike before suffering the fatal blow. His face and neck are red and sweating, and his T-shirt looks like a powdery, sugar-coated lemon drop that's probably attracted the hummingbirds, perhaps the explanation for his wild behavior in the garden. Willis tries to steer the boy back to the hospital. He wants to calm the boy before Dr. Renn arrives. Before the boy's father finds him like this. Before the boy can trigger a re-emergence of *Charlie*, wiping out thirty days of hard-won epiphanies and promises. "Let's go sit in the garden."

When Willis reaches for the boy's arm, the boy jerks out of reach. "Fuck your garden, fuck all of it. I hope it *all* dies." It's the emphasis on *all* that jolts Willis's heart like a man just resuscitated by a defibrillator.

"They didn't believe me—nobody believed anything I wrote in my essay about this summer. My stepmother called me a liar. Dr. Renn said I was writing to escape reality—that it's time I accept the consequences of the letter to Dad. My dad wouldn't even back me—said I had to prove I wasn't making it all up." The boy shakes a fist at Willis. He shouts that Dr. Renn called Maintenance and nobody there knew of *Willis, the man with one arm*. "So, I said I could prove it. Only I couldn't prove it because I couldn't find you. Couldn't even find Teana to back me up. The one time I need you and you're not here for me." He lunges toward Willis and pushes hard against his chest, and Willis, who any other time would be stone-mountain strong, absorbs the full brunt of the boy's warrior-self and stumbles backward. "The others are laughing at me," the boy says. "They're saying I'm the one that should be up there." The boy points skyward toward the barred windows of the dark north tower. "You've made me look like a crazy idiot. And now you're going to fix this."

The boy turns his back on Willis and storms up the hill toward the garden, no doubt expecting Willis to follow what sounds eerily like an order from *Charlie*. The screech of the hawk garners Willis's attention, and he sees that the hawk is flying in a darting, unnatural pattern. When the hawk swoops downward, Willis believes for a moment that the hawk is simply eager for the boy's attention, possibly for another biscuit feeding.

The hawk loves this boy.

This boy loves the hawk.

Of course, all this is wishful thinking because Willis knows in that way he has known all along that *this* is the probability he had hoped he and the boy would avoid. This was the probability that first revealed itself to him months earlier while he sat in Dr. Renn's office, searching for understanding—the same probability that struck him so hard several days later in Teana's cafeteria that he'd had to steady himself against the janitorial cart.

But wish always for the most benevolent outcome, and then accept what comes as the most benevolent outcome for ALL.

Willis looks back up the hill in time to see the hawk strike the boy's head. The boy shrieks, waves his arms, and then pumps his fists. "Get away from me, you crazy bird."

Again, Phoebe appears from nowhere, this time like a white marble sculpture that has been lowered in the middle of the garden he co-created for her what now seems lifetimes ago. From here, it's difficult to tell where the edges of her white gown separate from the enormous bushes behind her laden with white gardenia blossoms. She is crowned with a stirring kaleidoscope of curious circus-flying hummingbirds. Of course, they know her and love her already. They have been anticipating this moment for eons because Willis has willed it, created it within his mind, and shared with them the story of how he and Phoebe met, how they knew in a single hello-goodbye kiss that they had always known one another and would forever know and love one another in a way that would expand on their capacity for Compassion and Forgiveness.

"Go away," the boy shouts as he fights off more attacks by the screeching hawk.

And then Awareness dumps like cold lead into Willis's heart. He realizes now why the hawk, relentless, is fighting with the boy. In a single flash, Willis sees he's been standing so close to the Monet that while he could appreciate the beauty and power and intention within each brush stroke, he was too close to fully appreciate the meaning of the Divine Masterpiece. From this distance, watching the boy being chased by the hawk up the hill toward Phoebe and the garden, Willis is gaining impressions he wishes to deny. For while the strokes of the Monet blend brilliantly and vibrantly together for their proper intention, they do so now over the final shattering of Willis's heart. For a moment, he still tries to deny what he's known all along.

"No!" Willis cries aloud. "Haven't I given enough? *Why must this be so?*"

Is it ever wise to wish against the now obvious most benevolent outcome?

Willis knows the answer: while many will give, some will give all in service of the best and highest good for All.

And so it is. And so it begins.

The boy has finally reached the edge of the garden. He stops abruptly, and the hawk shrieks and swoops again for another aerial assault on the boy who has, for some reason, turned himself into an easy, unmovable ground target for the hawk. The hawk strikes hard at the boy's head, and still the boy does not move. The hawk returns, striking the boy again, and then takes its leave—soaring upward and westward over the Cooper VA.

Not since that moment in the 71st field evacuation hospital in Pleiku when Willis shamefully realized that the bounty on his head was responsible for leading the Viet Cong all the way to Pleiku and to Phoebe has Willis felt this helpless. This Awareness, too, he must allow and accept—even as the second uprising now appears over the garden. The butterfly-warrior-souls are ascending. Shape-shifting into a slow-moving vapor of color, they, too, drift westward as if being pulled by the wake of the Cooper's hawk.

Of course, Willis should be overcome with Joy. Of course, he grasps that the boy's Awakening will one day usher in a new elegance of consciousness. The boy is here for the Knowing. The Knowing will change the world.

Still, Willis cannot help but trudge head down up the slope. The dry brittle lawn crunches beneath his feet weighted with dread. The usual humming vibrations linked to the life force within the Cooper VA have been benevolently stilled for him by the stadiums of soul-gathering on the other side of the veil who wish Willis to hear only that the boy is calling over and over from the Nothingness.

Willis! Willis! Willis!

When Willis finally reaches the edge of the garden, he looks up to face the destructive consequence of the boy's Free-will probability that has destroyed the garden. And this is when the boy named Eli finally turns to face the man named Willis, and from the Nothingness Willis hears—*Oh my god, Willis! Can you ever forgive me?*

River-rivulets of blood from the aerial assaults of the hawk are sliding freely down the boy's face and neck, and are disappearing under the round collar of his T-shirt. The boy's horror-stricken expression reveals the death-and-destruction conclusion of a story that was long ago written for this day. With a landslide of Guilt and Regret bearing down—boulders gaining wipe-out speed and strength—the boy throws open his arms to accept the punishment he deserves from his teacher.

The sight of Phoebe finally standing among the drooping gardenias and roses and of the bleeding boy with his mouth open and slack and unable to create physical sound above the roar of Guilt—the boy's outstretched arms and Vulnerability—*these* are the two final keys that were needed to unlock that mysterious fifth chamber within Willis's heart.

Out pours the Greatest Flood of Compassion the World has Ever Known.

Willis rushes forward, his right arm extending, reaching for the boy. He takes that final step and locks the boy within an embrace that confirms what Willis only now recognizes as the Oneness-Remembering of who they truly are, were, and ever will be to one another after this Awakening.

And on the other side of the veil, the soul-gatherings within thousands of astral stadiums rise as One and cheer! And cheer!

This is the awakening *we* have anticipated for a thousand lifetimes—an awakening that had to include Phoebe and her gifts. You see, Willis may have dug the holes for her when she couldn't, and seeded them with the Potential she wouldn't, but Phoebe was always the catalyst, the co-creator of this Monet garden that once teemed with new-life possibilities, and as Willis consoles the sobbing boy in his arms, he smiles over at Phoebe. Never has she appeared more beautiful or more benevolent than in this moment with her arms outstretched in compassionate, yet utterly futile, attempts to catch each tiny hummingbird as it falls dead from the sky.

EPILOGUE

WILLIS HAWKINS, III
U.S. ARMY
VIETNAM

DEC. 12, 1950
AUG 21, 1971

SOME GAVE ALL

READING GUIDE

1. Beginning with the title, *Cooper's Hawk* can be described as richly layered in symbolism, metaphor, allusions, and allegory. What are the multiple implications behind the title, alone?

2. In the first paragraph, Willis is waiting on the sunrise to expose his cleaning mishaps, and reflects that a "second chance to fix a mistake is a gift." How does this theme of second chances resonate throughout the novel?

3. What are the many ways the author has revealed bird imagery to support various themes? How does each bird image or reference—whether a name or actual type of bird—specifically correlate to theme?

4. To most, Willis is invisible. Why is it that only Phoebe, the boy, Teana, the bearded screaming veteran on the psych ward, and the hawk and hummingbirds are able to "see" Willis? As a nurse, Phoebe whispers to each dying patient, "I see you." What is the significance of being seen, or not being seen? How has invisibility supported Willis throughout this narrative?

5. Who is the narrator of this story? How does the author's use of 1st person-plural point of view shape the story?

6. As Willis prepares for and contemplates the arrival of the troubled boy, Phoebe finally cracks under the pressure of flashbacks from Vietnam—flashbacks involving a boy in trouble and her role in saving him. How are the two references interrelated throughout the narrative?

7. Beyond his Native American heritage, what other assumptions or references might lead one to consider that Willis is less than a hundred percent Native American? What role, if any, does race and caste play regarding outcomes for various characters?

8. What is the novel's message regarding the difference between naming and labeling? What references support this?

9. Much attention has been devoted throughout the novel to the cardinal directions of north, south, east, and west with little, if any, explanation. What does a reader gain from the omission of specific explanations? What personal interpretations might the reader apply to each mention? For example, why do escaping patients of the psych ward always run east toward the cemetery? Why is the psych ward located in the north tower? At the end of the story, why do the Cooper's hawk and warrior-butterfly-souls depart for the west?

10. Likewise, how might one interpret the novel's messages regarding choices of left versus right? What symbolic messages can be associated with the loss of Willis's left arm, as opposed to his right? What symbolic advantage does Willis gain from only having use of his right arm, and what references throughout the novel support this?

11. The novel references symbolism from every major religion and spiritual belief. Identify references to Christianity, to Islam, to Buddhism, to Sufism, to Tao, to Shamanism, and to other spiritual beliefs. How do these specific references support various themes? How do they support one another, and the novel as a whole?

12. How is color used symbolically throughout the novel? Why would Willis ask, "When did all you nurses stop wearing white?" And why would this question cause Phoebe such hilarity? Why might the psych ward uniforms be gray? What colors are associated with the boy? With other characters?

13. What is the novel's overarching message regarding war, authoritarianism, and abuses of power? What repeating patterns from history are revealed within *Cooper's Hawk?* How does *Cooper's Hawk* support or challenge beliefs regarding war's impact on returning military servicemembers, their families, and the transition to civilian life?

14. Symbolically, water is associated with emotions. What water references within the novel support this symbolism?

15. How are examples of death and rebirth—figurative and literal—portrayed as inexplicably interwoven throughout the novel?

16. Nature plays an obvious role in Willis's plan to heal Phoebe and the boy, but why would Willis choose to employ the aid of a Cooper's hawk and hundreds of hummingbirds?

17. How does the setting of the Cooper VA, National Cemetery, and Blue Ridge Mountains influence the storyline?

18. What is the novel's message regarding the acceptance of our personal gifts and their connection between art and the co-created Self? What is the significance of using Monet as a reference to the garden Willis plants for Phoebe?

19. Why might Willis have chosen Desire as the only word to leave behind for Colonel Condor in the psych ward?

20. What assumptions might one conclude from the ending of *Cooper's Hawk?* What beliefs or values appear to be supported? How might the provocative and resonating final image of Phoebe and the hummingbirds be interpreted?

21. Throughout the novel, time is referenced as irrelevant— as nothing more than a construct. Yet the novel occasionally references a specific time or uses numbers as markers of time. Why? And how does the epilogue support the novel's overall message regarding the irrelevancy of linear time?

Q & A WITH
COOPER'S HAWK
AUTHOR TRACY CROW

Q: *What was the inspiration for* Cooper's Hawk*?*

TC: I would have to write an entirely new book, a memoir this time, to fully express all that inspired *Cooper's Hawk*, but the simplest, most direct answer is this: After three months of excruciating nerve pain on the right side of my body that had baffled a slew of doctors, I sought help from my neighbor, Novella, a licensed massage therapist who, as it turns out, specializes in this type of nerve pain. I had only met Novella and her husband Sam once since moving down our rural county road from them more than two years earlier. That first *chance* meeting had been over a dog that someone had abandoned at the top of my driveway. The dog had been there for several days before I noticed it. As a writer who works from home, I often go days, even a week or more, without leaving the property. So, when I finally did leave, I discovered this abandoned dog at the top of my 750-foot driveway. As I was posting a cardboard makeshift *Found Dog* sign in the yard, Sam drove by, slowed, and backed up. By this point, I'd already stashed the dog in my kennel in the backyard with food and water to keep her safe. I thought, or was hoping, Sam was backing up to claim the dog. Instead, he introduced himself and said that he and his wife had noticed the dog for several days and had decided to adopt her if she were still in my driveway that day. They came over together that evening, and left with the dog. After confirming with a veterinarian that the stray hadn't been microchipped with information about her owners and true home, they named her Phoebe. Phoebe was the magic catalyst that brought the three of us together.

But I didn't see them again for several months, not until the mysterious nerve pain that finally led me to Novella for help. After a few therapeutic sessions, Novella said she had something to share with me. Apparently, she said, I was to write a book about a man named Willis, a military veteran back from the war, and whose story involved the VA. She provided a couple of other descriptors that I won't share, but I made it clear that day that I was not going to write another military book, or a story about a man named Willis. She looked perplexed, so I offered to help her write the book. I said, "Besides, Willis didn't come to *me* with his story, he came to you." I meant this as a metaphysical joke—clearly Novella, who I'd already begun to identify with shaman-healing qualities, believed she was receiving a story from a man named Willis.

A few months later during another appointment, she mentioned Willis again, saying she'd been journaling all sorts of information about him and his life. And I turned this around on her as evidence of, "See? If Willis wanted me to write his story, he'd be sharing all that with me. It's your story to write, and I'll gladly help." Again, she looked perplexed.

Another couple of months later, now six or seven months since her first mention of Willis, she nudged again. Again, I refused. And again, she looked perplexed.

But a few days afterward, I was vacuuming the house on a Saturday morning, when I had a thought about Willis and Novella: *What would a book about Willis look like?* And that's when the entire story of *Cooper's Hawk* fluttered into consciousness—from the opening to the final image. When I saw that final image with the hummingbirds, I burst in tears and sat down in the living room. "No—I won't do that," I said aloud. "Why would any writer do that?" And I bawled my eyes out.

But now I had a *Willis* story of my own.

This was still six weeks from completion of *It's My Country Too* with my co-author, Jerri Bell, but soon as we shipped off the manuscript, I started writing *Cooper's Hawk*. The writing experience was the most blissful I've ever experienced. I tell everyone, I just showed up at five-thirty every morning for six weeks and tapped the keys on my laptop. Most of the time I had no idea what I'd written until I went back to review it for errors. And there were hardly any.

And for those six weeks, I kept following the magical strings of synchronicity that appeared every day. When I got stuck during the funeral scene for George Plover, I sensed something was about to change for Willis, but I didn't know what. I had a dentist appointment that morning, and during my dental cleaning, I mentally received the download of the entire scene and nearly choked on laughter as the dental tech was trying to clean my teeth. Like Willis in that moment,

I hadn't seen what Dove Jennings was about to reveal. That evening while feeding dinner to the dogs, I glanced out the window and discovered a mourning dove walking back and forth along the sidewalk that connects our driveway to the front door. I had never seen a mourning dove on our ten-acre property. Heard plenty of them, sure, but had never seen one. And now a mourning dove was strutting up and down the sidewalk at dusk—as if Dove Jennings was reminding me that I'd left him hanging in the middle of a sentence at George Plover's eulogy. Instead of waiting until the next morning's five-thirty writing session, I dashed to my office and wrote the scene as fast as I could.

As Novella and I would later discover, the story that Willis downloaded to me isn't the exact story he downloaded to Novella. In some ways, her version is much better. In some ways, mine is. But there's no denying that we were both receiving downloads of a similar story from the same source because of undeniable similarities.

Q: *What is your favorite scene?*

TC: Ugh...that's so hard, and even feels unfair in some way to choose one over another. I'll share that one of my favorites is the scene with the black snake, because this was in a sense co-created with Novella (and Willis!). And it happened like this just a few weeks before I began writing the book:

I'd had a dream one night about digging up an enormous chunk of raw tourmaline. The tourmaline was jagged, but with a black mirror finish. Actually, I should explain here that I didn't even know it was called tourmaline until I searched online and found several photos that looked exactly like what

I'd unearthed in the dream. So, this was how I discovered black tourmaline, and that black tourmaline is supposed to have protective metaphysical powers. But later that morning, I also discovered a black snake, at least eight feet long, on my back porch. Any other time in my life I would have been terrified, but I wasn't this time for some strange reason, at least not after I managed to get all four dogs inside. I took a broom and gently nudged the snake away from the porch, but he kept returning. Round after round we went, with me pleading with him to visit the front yard instead.

I finally drove him, nudging with the broom, from the porch and the back fenced yard, and he eventually took refuge in a nearby bed of bushes, disappearing under low the ground covering. As I walked up the steps to the porch, feeling victorious, I remembered the little wren's nest that was tucked under the fern fronds in the large blue urn on our porch. I determined the snake must have been going for the wren's eggs. I was congratulating myself, too, on saving the wren's eggs, when the large head of *another* black snake popped up from under the fern fronds of that blue urn. This time I screamed, "No!" And this time I was more than a little firm with my broom handling of snake number two, and greatly agitated the poor thing. The snake kept trying to climb up the broom toward me, and I kept trying to push, shove, this snake down the steps and toward the backyard. But this one was even more stubborn than the first.

Reminded of snake number one, I glanced toward that bed of bushes and saw that he was returning!

At this point, I was beginning to feel a little like Indiana Jones. This was nuts. I kept telling myself that I was supposed to stay cool, that I was being taught something, that the metaphor of snake and its symbolic transmutation were flooding my thoughts for a reason, but the overriding thought was still to save what might be left of the wren's nest of eggs.

Fortunately, when snake number one found snake number two, they slid off together under the nearby ground covering. I never saw them again. I will say they were both incredibly beautiful. Their scales were shiny mirror black, and I later connected them to the dream of the raw black tourmaline I'd unearthed. When I shared all this excitement in a phone call with my girlfriend in Florida, and mentioned tourmaline, she gasped. "What did you just say?" I repeated *black tourmaline*. She said, "You're not going to believe this, but while online this morning, an ad for a necklace popped up and it reminded me of you, so I just ordered it for you. You'll receive it in a day or so. It's raw black tourmaline." We both let out a collective scream. She had never heard of tourmaline before that morning either.

Novella happened to be camping with Sam in upstate New York that day. I sent her a text about the encounter and bemoaned that the snake had eaten all the wren's eggs. And she returned the text: "Maybe ask yourself why you think the wren deserves more protection than the snake." BAM! I knew this would somehow work its way into *Cooper's Hawk*. The next morning, she sent another text while eating her breakfast of eggs: "At least the snake was ethically hunting for its food."

So, because of the tourmaline dream, the sudden appearance of two black snakes, the wren's nest and eggs, and Novella's always provocative insights, this scene in the book between Willis and the boy feels especially meaningful and co-created.

Q: *Do you feel changed in any way because of this book, how it came to you, how it was written? Didn't you write this in six weeks?*

TC: Yes, I completed the book in six weeks. Two weeks into the writing, I had this sense that the book was supposed to be finished in four more weeks. I said aloud, "I can't write a novel in six weeks!" And what I immediately heard back, in my mind, was, "You're not writing a novel…you're writing a *novella*." All this had happened while I was walking between my office and the kitchen, and when I heard *novella*, and thought of how persistent dear-friend *Novella* had been about me writing this book about Willis, I stopped in the hallway and busted out laughing. "Of course, I can finish a *novella* in six weeks." And I did.

Do I feel changed? Very much so. Writing has always felt like a job, tedious at times. This writing, however, was blissful. Joyful. I couldn't wait to return to the writing every day. I felt rejuvenated after each writing session, too, not drained as I did with previous writing projects. But probably what changed for me the most was how this book developed my wide-angle awareness. How bread crumbs of synchronicity were transforming into strings of synchronicity, and how much easier my life was flowing through each day as long as I followed the synchronicity. So much synchronicity that at times I'd just laugh out loud at how obvious it all was, and joke, "Uh-huh, I see what you're doing there! High five, Higher Self!" Much as I fought this my entire life until writing this book, I know now—we truly are eternal, we truly are creating our own reality, we truly are so much more than most of us think we are, and we truly are connected to one another through thought.

Q: *Do you have a favorite line?*

TC: Without hesitation, it's "Accept your gifts."

Q: *Can you share why?*

TC: In 2008, I attended a meditation event—my first. Two yogis dressed in white roamed the large chapel while all of us sat with eyes closed, meditating—I didn't even know what meditating was then—and listening to hypnotic music. As I remember it, they roamed the chapel three times, pausing behind each of us, and you could always tell, or I could anyway, when one of them moved behind you because of the energy change. I could feel the energy behind me, even though no one touched me or whispered anything.

But during the final round, I heard a loud voice say, "Accept your gifts," and I had to resist the urge to whirl around because I realized just as quickly that the voice had been inside my head, my own mind. But this voice sounded sure and clear. Not at all like the typical monkey-brain chatter that happens in there.

I walked to my car afterward, thinking, *What gifts?*

I called my Florida friend on the drive home, told her what happened, and joked, "I'd gladly accept my gifts if I just knew what they were!"

And eight years later, maybe even to the day, I was tapping out, "Accept your gifts" in *Cooper's Hawk.*

Q: *Who is Willis really? Do you know?*

TC: Throughout the writing of *Cooper's Hawk*, I merely thought of Willis as imagination—a creative swirling energetic vortex between Novella and me and obviously someone on the other side of the veil. One day, I asked Novella if she ever thought we'd discover who Willis really is, and her expression shocked me. A look of *Don't you know?*

That evening in my bedroom, I asked aloud, "OK, Willis, who are you?" And what I immediately heard back rattled me at first. In that same loud, clear, sure voice that had years earlier declared, "Accept your gifts," what I heard this time was…

You

ABOUT THE AUTHOR

TRACY CROW, a former Marine Corps officer and college journalism and writing professor, is president/ CEO of MilSpeak Foundation, a 501(c) 3 public charitable organization that supports the creative arts endeavors of military servicemembers, veterans, and family members. She is the author or editor of five books: the newly released popular history, *It's My Country Too: Women's Military Stories from the American Revolution to Afghanistan,* with co-author, Jerri Bell; the award-winning, critically acclaimed military memoir, *Eyes Right: Confessions from a Woman Marine*; the conspiracy thriller, *An Unlawful Order* under her pen name Carver Greene; the breakthrough writing text, *On Point: A Guide to Writing the Military Story;* and the anthology, *Red, White, and True: Stories from Veterans and Families, WWII to Present.*

CPSIA information can be obtained
at www.ICGtesting.com
Printed in the USA
FFOW03n1018110418
46230408-47594FF

9 781943 258635